D 40

DENIM RYDER

DENIM RYDER

•

Stone Wallace

AVALON BOOKS
NEW YORK

Published by Thomas Bouregy & Co., Inc.
160 Madison Avenue, New York, NY 10016

Library of Congress Cataloging-in-Publication Data

Wallace, Stone, 1957–
Denim Ryder / Stone Wallace.
p. cm.
ISBN 978-0-8034-7750-6 (acid-free paper) 1. Revenge—Fiction. I. Title.
PR9199.4.W3424D46 2010
813'.6—dc22

2009024260

PRINTED IN THE UNITED STATES OF AMERICA
ON ACID-FREE PAPER
BY HADDON CRAFTSMEN, BLOOMSBURG, PENNSYLVANIA

Dedicated with Love to Cindy
"The Story Fairy"

"All the vast labors of America have been inspired
and made possible by its masterpiece:
its energetic woman."

—Paul Bourget, 1895

"For the woman with outdoor propensities and a taste
for roughing it there is no life more congenial
than that of the saddle and rifle . . ."

—Evelyn Cameron, 1906

Prologue

The Place: The Tellahu Desert
The Location: The American Southwest
The Year: 1862

They had laid the body of his wife before him, her corpse spread-eagle in the sand and stripped of her fine clothes and undergarments. Viciously shorn of the long golden locks she had worn with such pride. She had been murdered by the younger warriors of the tribe, and as the man could detect from the agonized grimace frozen upon her features, savagely tortured before death in its mercy had freed her. Now she lay as carrion, pickings for the buzzards that hovered and swooped about him. For long, seemingly endless days he could no longer remember, the man had stood lashed to the post, watching numbly as the corpse was dissected under the relentless attacks of the flying predators.

Helpless before this gruesome sight, the man awaited his own death.

His shirt had been blade-ripped to tatters while deep cuts had been dug into the flesh of his shoulders, arms, and upper torso. The blazing rays of the daytime sun had seared into the gaping wounds until each gash had become encrusted with congealed blood. His face was raw and blistered, his cheeks streaked a chalky white from tears that he could no longer cry. His eyes were now dry and burning, barely able to focus against the extreme desert glare. His only defense against the greed of the buzzards' hunger were his shouts, parched and ever-weakening as his last ounces of strength surrendered to the heat and his own need for water and nourishment.

He prayed for the release of death before their return.

He did not know when they would come—but they *would* be back. And unless death claimed him first, he knew that their final justice would be without mercy.

The suffocating desert heat and both the sight and stench of the decomposing body of what had once been his wife made him physically sick. He'd vomited what little remained in his stomach, but still his body heaved—wrenching dry heaves. No matter how hard he tried to avert his eyes, his gaze kept returning to the corpse stretched out only a few feet before him. What remained of it. The woman he had loved and taken into his arms as his bride no longer resembled anything human. Except perhaps in the delirium of his mind. There he remembered her beauty. The closeness they had shared, his promises of a better life . . . and now what was most painful to him—her belief in his words. He had not only failed her, he had betrayed her. No matter what end the Apache intended for him, it could never compare to the torment he now brought upon himself.

How much longer? his thoughts pleaded as he cast his gaze into the cloudless skies. He could hardly know the answer to that question any more than he knew how long he had been subjected to this torture. Sunrises blurring into sunsets. Merciful periods of blackouts, becoming more frequent now. And yet he always returned from them, as if the Apache gods would not permit such an easy end to his ordeal.

On this day he returned to awareness by the sound of hoofbeats racing in the distance. He flashed open his eyes and squinted against the blinding white glare.

He saw them.

A small group of riders. He made himself believe they were of his own people, coming to rescue him. Overwhelmed with the thought of his freedom, he attempted to call out to them. Only his throat was so parched all that issued from his lips was a throaty rasp.

They were an army patrol, and they would set him free. Through the shimmering desert haze he swore he could see their cavalry uniforms. Though not a man given to religion, he began to mouth a silent prayer.

He could see their proud horses galloping in formation across the hard, cracked surface of the sand. He tried with what little effort he could muster to loosen himself from the rawhide binding that secured him to the post. But even this feeble effort quickly proved exhausting. He would need their assistance. Still, he managed to keep his head erect in acknowledgment of their approach. To let them know that he was still alive.

And then . . . the colors of the riders changed. Suddenly there were no uniforms. He blinked several times to clear himself of this cruel hallucination.

But the truth became known to him. . . .

It was not a cavalry patrol that dismounted. The men were Apache warriors, come to perform their final justice. The warriors were bare-chested, wearing only breech-cloths, not armed with the rifles with which the man well knew they had been supplied. Instead each warrior brandished the bow and arrows they favored as the method for executing their enemies.

He forced himself to stand firm against the binding as the warriors silently took up positions just several yards before him.

He took a final look down at the pitiful remains of his wife. He wondered with almost his last clear thought if within these next few moments they would be reunited. And if so, would she be forgiving to him? He was barely able to mouth "God forgive me" before the first arrow pierced deep into his shoulder. He winced as its serrated head tore through ligament and muscle. Then he braced himself for the next assault. He watched the four young Apache warriors slowly fit arrows into their bows and take aim in his direction.

He managed to pull himself upright and stood in defiance as one after the other they let loose their bowstrings.

Each of the arrows found its mark, lodging into his side and belly. He knew that any one shot could have killed him, could have brought an end to his misery, but the warriors were not quite ready to grant him a quick death.

The immediate pain was agonizing, but he quickly became numb to it with the realization that soon it would be over.

His last thoughts were of the baby daughter he had hardly known. The child who had been brought into his life and raised by him. Although he hoped she would forever be spared the terrible truth behind their death, he made himself strong for her memory.

"Kill me if you're gonna!" he somehow found the voice to cry before the second volley of arrows struck and he slumped forward against his binding, dead.

Chapter One

The Desert

She rode her mount onward through the blistering midday heat, through shale-littered desert terrain rarely ventured by any white man, let alone woman—driven forward by a determination to learn the truth.

Her destination was the town of Prosperity, where she alone would seek justice against the man who years before had betrayed her parents to the Apaches.

She'd followed a long trail, beset by forces of nature over which only God had control. She knew her trek north across the western edge of the Tellahu Desert would prove difficult, exposing her both to real and imagined dangers. But her will and purpose were strong and she would not turn back from what she had set out to do.

The Apache still roamed these parts, which was why she maintained her trail along the parched, desolate flatlands, keeping a secure distance during the daylight hours from the eastern ridge of mountains where the foothills would provide cooling shade and protection from the harsh changes in climate . . . but could also possibly lead her into an Indian ambush. For, unlike her, the Apache knew the land well.

While she rode in the open, making herself visible to enemy eyes, she knew it was vital that she keep her view unimpeded. She could see an attack coming from any direction, and she knew that would give her the advantage and the chance to outrun it.

Still, a sense of foreboding rode with her during her journey, not eased by the monotony of the table-flat, far-stretching landscape . . . or the uncertain weather, which could shift suddenly into frightening extremes. The conditions during the first two days of her anticipated three-day desert trek had been anything but agreeable. Stifling hot days, almost claustrophobic, where the sweat would run down her face in rivulets, dripping into her eyes and blurring her vision, already strained from the sand-reflected glare of the sun. She would attempt to cool herself by unbuttoning her shirt as she rode, hoping perhaps to prompt a breeze. But her effort provided little relief. The searing heat was often coupled with hot, stinging winds that prickled her flesh. In contrast, the nights became bitterly cold, against which her blankets provided little warmth. She'd brought along sufficient water to sustain both herself and her mount, but she'd used up too much during the early part of her journey so that now rationing became necessary. Yet even with this decision, her supply was quickly becoming exhausted. She drank little herself, more concerned with the handsome bay-colored Mustang she had raised from a foal, whom she had named Daybreaker. She rode her trail with the stubborn optimism of coming upon sources of water from which to replenish her canteens; instead she was discouraged to discover only arroyos—wrinkled indentations where once rain-fed streams had flowed.

She learned fast that the desert was a study in extremes. As she set up camp during those first nights, daring to venture east into the protection of the foothills, she refused to light a fire that might betray her presence to a lurking enemy, and instead braced herself as best she could against the cold—but a dry cold against clear skies that foretold yet another day of oppressive heat unrelieved by any sign of rain. The Tellahu Desert is the one place on God's earth where a person experiences total isolation. It is a lonely land, haunting in its environment and illusion. The silence is prolonged and hangs heavy over the bleak landscape. Every sound that does occur approaches with a startling suddenness. The land itself is unrelenting in its desolation, often creating strange images that can deceive the brain. Devoid of even the barest essentials needed for survival, this westernmost region of the Tellahu Desert had driven more than one traveler to madness—and death. The girl had taken precautions for this part of her journey, but as the hours and days crept by slowly, and her progress likewise slowed, even she realized how physically and mentally unprepared she was against this most formidable adversary. It was only through the sheer grit that had seen her overcome other hardships that the girl continued on.

Of all her perils, both real and imagined, it was the consuming isolation that most affected her. She was the type of girl who had always preferred solitude, yet she found herself becoming overwhelmed by her aloneness and spent much of her time talking to Daybreaker—if really to herself.

Towards midafternoon on what she saw as her final day's journey, she began to sense a gradual shifting in the weather—imperceptible yet tangible. Not a coming of rain, for which she had hoped, but something more . . . quietly ominous. One sign she immediately recognized was that the sky had taken on a peculiar hue, not consistent with the midday hour. Daybreaker too was acting strangely, his acute senses aware of what was ahead, receptive to the electricity that suddenly charged the air. He grew agitated, halting, tugging against the reins. The girl spoke comfortingly to him, trying to calm his fears, and the soothing recognition of her voice seemed to settle the horse—but for how long? The girl knew for a certainty that, unlike an attack from the Apaches, they could never outdistance whatever it was that was coming—and she feared she knew exactly what that was. Her primary concern now was to find protection.

She focused on the eastern foothills, off in the distance. She was reluctant to wander too far off her daytime trail as precious time would be lost, but as the unnatural stillness that had descended upon the earth broke with those first gusts of wind, she knew she had no other choice but to go to where she might find protection from the weather.

The storm hit before dusk. The skies turned a swirling, ashen gray as a northern wind whipped up mighty gales of sand and dust. It came with a fury, quickly blackening the skies and choking the air with violent lashings of grit. The girl hurriedly threw on her frock coat, turning up the collar. She tipped her Stetson low over her forehead, tightening the drawstring under her neck, and drew her kerchief up over the lower half of her face to shield herself from the stinging, suffocating gusts.

The girl tried to drive Daybreaker forward, but the animal's strength and tenacity were fast becoming tested. Each step he took against the assaulting winds was an effort.

"Come on, Daybreaker," Denim urged, gently yet firmly. "We gotta find ourselves cover. We got to."

The wind howled furiously. The blasting sand bit into her like lashes from a whip. She was fast becoming disoriented, losing her sense of direction. Her kerchief and Stetson kept out most of the sand that swept into her face, but Daybreaker had no such protection and she feared that the relentless blasts might choke him.

But she refused to give up hope, no matter what they were riding against. Her eyes were red and burning, her field of vision now limited, distancing not much beyond the lead of her horse. Yet she struggled on, searching the eastern ridges for refuge.

Her horse was sluggish in his pace.

"We ain't gonna be givin' up, Daybreaker," she shouted with a burst of determination intended for herself as well as her horse. "We're gonna make it through this, boy."

But she knew the bitter truth. It could have all been over then. And perhaps she might have surrendered to that inevitability . . . if a voice had not suddenly spoken to her. Words offered to her from a cherished memory.

If one is chosen for a purpose in life, no obstacle, mortal or otherwise, can stand in the way of seeing its completion.

She knew who had spoken those words. And now as she needed it most, she recognized the truth in them. She had established that purpose and was now sure that she was not intended to die here in the dry desert sands. She was meant to see that this challenge was just one more test to determine her own strengths. A strength she would surely need once she rode into the town of Prosperity.

And so she pressed on, her heart breaking as she was forced to push her loyal mount past the point of endurance. Yet she understood that if they were to survive there was no other way. Even as the air grew colder, and thinner, her lungs constricting, requiring her to inhale shallow breaths, she told herself that she would live to fulfill her purpose.

Her concern remained with Daybreaker. He was growing ever more weakened, almost buckling under the strain. The girl was fearful; she could see that his only chance of going on was without carrying additional weight. She swung herself off the saddle and, gently guiding her horse by the bridle, plodded on foot through the blowing winds and drifting sands.

They finally made it to the foothills and Denim found what looked like a secure spot in an outcropping of rocks along the lower ridge. She felt she'd be safe there since it was doubtful any Apache would venture out into the storm. But she planned to remain on her guard. The rocks provided enough of a barrier to shelter Denim and her horse from the forward rush of the wind.

She struggled against the wind to remove a small blanket covering from the packsaddle. She tried to keep Daybreaker calm as she knotted the ends of the material loosely yet firmly around his head to protect his eyes from the merciless onslaught. She then drew her frock coat tightly around herself and set her body on the ground with her knees drawn up to her chest and her back pressed firmly against the rocks.

The storm went on.

The night was the longest of her life. The wind roared with a maddening intensity that never subsided, seeming to shake the earth beneath her. The lower gusts whistled eerily through the narrow cracks between the rocks. They sounded like the mournful ghostly cries of past travelers who had not survived their journey.

While she would be loathe to admit it, the girl was scared. Her only comfort was that Daybreaker stood nearby, firm in his purpose and protecting her even as he was blasted by sand-driven winds. The girl spoke to her companion throughout the night—again her words as much a reassurance to herself, as she had never before felt so vulnerable.

Toward dawn the fierce winds lessened, beginning to whisper and take on a slow calm. And finally, with the worst now over, the girl gave in to her fatigue and she dozed.

She awoke to a gentle snort close to her ear that immediately filled her with an unbounded relief and joy. Snapping open her eyelids she saw Daybreaker's face just inches from hers. To the girl it was the most beautiful face she had ever seen. The horse looked a little weather-beaten, lathered, but healthy and alert. She threw her arms around the animal's strong, firm neck, then pressed her cheek against the side of his face and stroked his mane, thankful that he had made it through their terrible ordeal.

"You're a strong one, Daybreaker," she cooed. "And I love you."

As she sat herself down to a quick breakfast of dried berries from her saddlebag and provided feed and only a little water for her horse, she felt a renewed confidence. The elements had worked against her, throwing her off her course, but even with valuable riding time lost to the storm, she was proud to acknowledge that she had not been bested.

Still, one fear would continue to travel with her—the one true terror that she fought hard not to dwell upon. And that was the threat of the ruthless and clever Apache. While she had chosen her trail knowing that Indian warriors rarely traveled this barren stretch of desert, the possibility existed that her lone and open figure could be spotted from afar, or that she could encounter a scout or renegade. Her protection was the six bullets she'd loaded into the chambers of the left-draw single-action .45 Colt in her gun belt and a capacity fifteen rounds in the magazine of the Winchester in the saddle boot under her leg. She was skilled at using both.

It was only a day later that the girl came to the border of the grasslands, an oasis of green set upon the land like a jewel. She cleansed the desert from her lungs with several deep breaths of the clean, pristine air.

And it was with relief, gratitude, and no small amount of pride at her own fortitude that she gently urged Daybreaker forward on the last leg of her journey. The desert wasteland was behind her.

Laurie Ryder, the girl who had established her reputation throughout the Southwest as "Denim Ryder," was a survivor.

Chapter Two

The Girl

The word that best described Denim Ryder was fetching. She was truly the desire of any man with whom she had shared an acquaintance: a long-legged beauty with an innocent, childlike face that belied her twenty-two years and the tough independence she carried with the assurance of her side arms. She wore her hair long: honey-blond strands swept off to the side, where it spilled loose over peach-smooth, delicate features further complemented by soft blue eyes as clear as the twilight skies, set in a perpetual expression of wonderment. Her full, petulant lips could widen into a dimpled smile so bright that it had stolen the heart of many a suitor. Denim was proud of her looks. ("It's like lookin' at your ma," her grandpa would often remark, shaking his head in admiration.) Yet she remained a contradictory girl. She refused to adopt the accepted wear of a proper woman, not having put on a dress since she was a child. Instead she preferred traditional ranch attire of tight-fitting blue jeans and a waist-length denim jacket or vest. Even her broad-brimmed, high-crowned cowboy Stetson was fashioned from the same material. It was her grandpa who had first called her "Denim," and the nickname stuck. It suited her just fine.

Denim Ryder was a girl who could hold her own. At a young age, bereft of playmates or the usual childhood amusements, she had taught herself to ride and later helped domesticate the wild breeds her grandpa would herd off the range. She possessed a natural affinity for horses. She took her share of bucks and tumbles, yet displayed a stubborn tenacity that eventually saw her break every bronco she'd ridden. While she'd never seen the inside of a classroom, she received her education in other ways: as a trick rider, performing at local events with Daybreaker, her reputation soon leading to a professional engagement on the Sam Abbott Wild West Circuit, whose shows traveled extensively throughout the Southwest. Showman Sam Abbott wasted no time capitalizing on her abilities and billed her prominently as "The West's Authentic Cowgirl."

Denim's skills were not limited to her impressive horsemanship. She'd spent long hours learning how to handle a gun: revolver or repeater rifle, becoming proficient as a left-handed sharpshooter. By the time she was sixteen, she could outdraw most men and hit repetitive bull's-eyes with a speed and accuracy that furthered her celebrity along the circuit.

That night, settled on the grasslands beside a cool, refreshing stream from which she and Daybreaker drank freely, Denim relaxed and anticipated her first truly restful sleep since starting off on her journey. She had traveled slow that day. Both she and Daybreaker were exhausted from their journey and travails in the desert, and Denim had set up camp come dusk. It was a glorious twilight: a mural of sun-edged purple clouds rolling against the deepening blue of the sky.

Denim soon drifted off to sleep under the soft glow of the stars. And, as she often did as a young girl before being tucked into bed by the one man she loved most of all, she comforted herself by reflecting on the special times spent with her grandpa. . . .

Her memory on this night was bittersweet.

She recalled a morning not long ago. She and her grandpa were up early rocking on the porch swing, moving in lazy rhythm to the squeaking hinges, both sharing the spectacular panaroma of another prairie sunrise. She would be leaving that morning to join up with Sam Abbott's troupe for a two-month tour in Mexico. For three years she had traveled seasonally with the show as the premier attraction, entertaining audiences with her equestrian acrobatics and fancy side-arm shooting. It was always an exciting time for Denim, but the long partings from her grandpa also filled her with sadness.

Leaving home this time would be particularly difficult.

What Denim particularly remembered about that morning was the tinkling of the wind chimes that hung over the porch. They were a gift from her grandpa—the only present that he'd ever given her, and it was a gift she cherished. It provided a soothing music in the gentle morning breeze, before the air stilled, and Denim could enjoy listening to them for hours.

She and Grandpa rarely spoke when enjoying this time together. Their thoughts alone provided a communion. Grandpa in particular had always been a man of few words. But when he had something to say, he meant it, and spoke with intent.

Grandpa was sipping on a cup of the strong coffee he had brewed himself when Denim took one of his aged yet still-rugged hands in hers and Grandpa didn't resist, an unusual gesture between two people who rarely displayed physical affection.

"You got somethin' to be tellin' me," he said gruffly.

Denim hesitated, then spoke quietly. "I won't be comin' right back after the tour this time."

Grandpa blinked, squinted slightly, but he remained silent.

"I aim to be ridin' up to Prosperity," Denim said straightly.

The old man gazed off into the horizon, toward the distant mountains and the burst of bright gold that crested their peaks.

"We both knew this day was comin'," Denim told him by way of explanation.

Grandpa finally shrugged and spoke without emotion. "I thought I knowed a lot of things. That we'd be clearin' the land of the Apaches. That laws'd come into place that'd protect decent folk from the likes of Brock Donovan." The old man gave his head a slow, sad shake, as if trying to erase a bad memory. "Nothin's changed." He sighed. "Maybe all I ever really knowed was what I wanted to believe."

"Don't be holdin' this agin me, Grandpa," Denim said softly. "And there ain't nothin' wrong with believin'. This country's still growin', you said it yourself. Folks have just given too much to others."

Grandpa sat reflectively, saying nothing.

"And I've grown too, Grandpa," Denim added in a peculiar tone.

The old man turned his head toward her. "That you have," he said quietly.

"And now . . . I gotta do what we both knew I was gonna do someday."

Denim waited for an acknowledgment that her grandpa did not offer.

She spoke firmly. "I gotta hear Brock Donovan tell me straight what he done."

"That man's never spoke an honest word in his life," Grandpa snorted.

"Grandpa, you raised me the best you know how. You looked after me and you protected me. You never wanted to tell me the truth 'bout my folks. But today I'm askin' you not to keep it from me anymore."

The old man pretended not to hear her. "Brock Donovan's *respectable* now," he said with just a note of contempt.

"What's respectable 'bout a thievin' murderer?" Denim said spitefully.

The old man shifted weary eyes toward his granddaughter. "He won't be havin' no dealin's with the likes of you."

"I lived my whole life not knowin' the truth," Denim argued.

Grandpa squinted. Then after a long period of quiet, as if trying to muster the courage to voice his thoughts, he said: "I knew it was wrong. I knew it." He abruptly fell silent, until his eyes reached into the corral and his face brightened. "Caillou was the first horse I ever broke. Named this here ranch after that steed."

Denim followed the old man's gaze into the sun-spilled gold of the corral, where only a few broken quarter horses remained. Bucks that even the old man knew he would never sell. Denim understood that it was sometimes difficult for her grandpa to accept that the days when he had been a youthful wrangler had long since passed. But she couldn't tell if this sudden reflection was a momentary reliving of those early years . . . or perhaps his way of avoiding a more painful memory.

"It's my right to know," Denim urged.

The old man's expression grew taut. He cupped one hand over the other and began massaging his knuckles, which were aching from arthritis.

"I reckon it is," he muttered. He shifted forward in his seat but kept his attention focused far off into the distance. "We lived a hard life, your grandma and me. But we never took from no one. What little we owned we worked for ourselves. And it was precious little. We was never obligin' to no man. Amy, your ma . . . we did the best we could fer her. But I reckon it was never enough. After your grandma died and with me bein' out on the range for long spells, well, we just kinda drifted aways from each other. She could never take to this kind of life, and I reckon under the circumstances I couldn't rightly blame her. Next thing I knew she's set to marry your pa. I reckon Cal Ryder was basically a good man. Came from good stock. It's just that things never seemed to go right for him. Your ma used to tell me that Cal was always courtin' her with the fancy talk. How he was gonna buy her things and take her to all the places she wanted to go. It's all what she wanted to hear, I reckon, and Cal was a smooth talker. After you was born, your pa got to gamblin' to keep all them promises he made to Amy. That's where he made the acquaintance of Brock Donovan. Donovan owned the most crooked gamblin' hall in Tombstone, and from what I figger, he leeched so much blood outta your pa that he could never pay off his debt. So Donovan worked out another arrangement. He put Cal to work for him, which I reckon is what he wanted all along." The old man halted and lowered his eyes to the porch. It was the longest speech Denim could ever remember him making.

But Denim could see how difficult it was for her grandpa

to be remembering. She allowed him a moment before gently urging him to continue.

The old man pulled a cloth from his pocket and coughed into it. He went on. "What people didn't know was that Brock Donovan kept friendly with the Apaches. During the early days of the wars he supplied 'em with cattle. Not from his herds. No, he was too smart to risk havin' his brand be recognized. Story goes that he hired renegades to rustle cattle outta Mexico. Y'see, he had his sights set on a prime stretch of grazin' land that the Indians held claim to. He made a deal with Cochise that promised him the land if he'd supply beef and guns to the tribe. The Indians knew they couldn't win this skirmish so givin' up their land was of no matter. More important to the Apaches was facin' their defeat with honor, not to be surrenderin' without a fight. Over a hundred fifty people was killed by the Chiricahua before the army moved in. Thing is, Donovan would never trust an Indian to keep his part of the bargain, and it was probably him who sent the soldiers against them. And it was then that Donovan covered his own trail by turnin' over some of his own people as an Apache 'peace offerin'—your ma an' pa among 'em."

Denim braced herself before asking: "What happened to 'em?"

Grandpa exhaled a heavy sigh. His eyes looked pained. "Don't know. They never recovered their bodies. Truth is, I don't want to know. But the Apaches have a way with torture, even among their own. Your folks and them others employed by Donovan was looked upon as traitors. The Apaches don't show no mercy to traitors." The old man grew quiet before he continued. "Brock Donovan's got his land now, made his money, and built his reputation. He's a man far away from his past. 'Respectable,' as I said. He's both powerful and he's protected. There's only a few of us left that knows about his double-dealin'. Donovan likes to cover his tracks. But I ain't afraid of him. And I've come to the point in my life where I'm plain bled dry of the need for revenge."

Denim responded increduously. "How can you say that knowin' what he's done?"

Grandpa merely shrugged. "Whatever's comin' to him will be the will of the Lord."

Denim's blue eyes widened. "I can't believe you really feel that way—after what he done to your daughter. My ma."

Grandpa replied without apology, "I ain't sayin' I can find it in myself to forgive the man. But the way I figger, I'm gonna be standin' before Him soon, and it ain't gonna do my soul much good to meet my Maker with a heart filled with hate."

Denim spoke with bitterness. "You'll stand before Him, Grandpa, also knowin' that a kind and forgivin' God might not judge Brock Donovan too harshly." Her temper flashed. "I hate him, Grandpa. I'll hate him forever. And a whole lot more than yer God ever will!"

The old man's eyes flashed angrily. "Don't you go

talkin' blasphemy, girl. No matter what my sins, I tried to bring you up in the ways of your grandma—to be respectful and God fearin'."

Denim spoke through pursed lips. "It don't seem right that only those who suffer should be fearin' of God."

Grandpa took another deep breath then settled back on the swing. He spoke thoughtfully. "This is a land where a man can go on killin', either by intent or indifference. People blame the Apache, but that ain't entirely right. It's survival gone bad. It's . . . people simply tryin' to stay alive. In my time I seen many a good man turn bitter mean. Not 'cause they was born that way, but because the land itself can turn agin you. In some folks that struggle to survive can turn a man's heart so black that soon he don't know no other way to live."

"But you, Grandpa . . . you never turned to that way of livin'," Denim remarked softly.

"No." The old man sighed. "Never did. That way of life wasn't my choosin'. Still, I done my share of things I ain't proud of."

"I just knowed you as a good man, Grandpa," Denim said with a timid smile.

The old man only faintly returned the smile.

After a spell, Grandpa furrowed his brow and went on. "Whatever my sins, I figger I paid for 'em when I lost my daughter. But the good Lord did for me what he don't always do for others. He gave me a second chance—with you. I raised you as my own, and I musta done a fair job. 'Cause you never once done wrong by me."

Denim's voice was subdued. "You know I was never what you expected of me."

The old man eyed her peculiarly. "No? And what was that? I made mistakes with your ma. My own fault, I reckon. But fact is . . . I always was kinda proud of what you done."

Denim found herself reacting with surprise at his rare acknowledgment of her accomplishments.

Then the old man snapped at her. "But it ain't right for a girl to be doin' what your aimin'—"

"I ain't a girl no more," Denim interjected firmly.

Grandpa grimaced and softened his tone. He scratched the white stubble on his chin. "No. I reckon not. Then you never was, was you? Lord, this land raised both you and your ma. You look so much like her, girl, and yet the two of you couldn't be more different."

Denim did not reply. She watched, astonished, as an emotion welled up in her grandpa that she had never witnessed before. It was in some ways easier for her to attribute his tears to the brutal honesty that one must face as he nears the closing days of his life. Perhaps a life unfulfilled—or a life of regret. But this unexpected show of emotion was not directed toward his own mistakes. In the quiet way by which he had lived his life, her grandpa was imparting to her a wisdom—a truth that he could embrace fully, but one that she might never appreciate until her own twilight years were upon her.

Denim knew it was time to go. She slid forward on the swing, rolled up the cuffs of her jeans, and pulled on her riding boots.

"I'd best be on my way," she said as she got up. She stood next to her grandpa for a moment, but he remained seated, his inward expression suggesting that he'd not heard her. Denim smiled sadly, then walked across to the barn to saddle Daybreaker. After several minutes the old man slowly rose and followed her into the barn.

He walked over beside her as she readied her horse. When Denim saw him, she could not resist laying a tender hand on his arm.

"I'll be back, Grandpa," she promised.

The old man feigned annoyance and halfheartedly pulled back his arm, though not enough to free himself entirely from her touch.

"I could never be tellin' you what to do anymore'n I could your ma," he grumbled, yet his tone was also strangely affectionate.

Denim looked at the old man and noticed how his eyes had become moist. He quickly wiped the tears away with a motion that suggested he'd merely gotten some dust in his eyes. She thought of how much she loved him, a love she had never been able to express in words. But she was sure he knew—and she also understood that he felt the same way. Denim knew how he cherished these special times when dawn broke over the mountains. Her setting out at this hour had always been difficult, as much for her grandpa as for herself. Maybe they had never shared the open affection she would have liked, but she accepted that this was just the type of man he was. A man born of the country: hard-skinned and proud. A good man, but not one given to displays of sentiment. She would ride out this morning without his giving her a hug or a kiss good-bye—or even an affectionate word. Instead she would carry with her on her journey the precious early morning memories of his stories and adventures—stories he told as much to himself as a reminder of a long-ago youth. But Denim also knew Grandpa was appreciative to have an ear with which to share these remembrances.

"You just take care of yourself," Grandpa said to her.

"I will." Denim smiled. "And you look after yourself 'til I get back." She paused, then said as an afterthought, "And don't be forgettin' Elena will be around in a few days to see if you need anything."

"Aww," Grandpa said dismissively, kicking back dirt with his boot heel.

Denim took Daybreaker by the reins and led him from the stall. She mounted her horse outside the barn. She was supplied and prepared for her trip, and the sun was already a bright guide to lead her onto her trail. Daybreaker seemed eager to get moving and Denim had to steady the animal. Then she gazed down at the the lined and weathered face of her grandpa.

The old man spoke bluntly. "Well, git if you have to."

Denim nodded. There was so much she wanted to say to him upon this leaving—and more in her heart that she feared she might never have the chance to tell him. But she firmly believed that he knew what she felt, and, while not acknowledged, it was a comfort to her.

"Good-bye, Grandpa," she said. She gave a wave, which

the old man returned, and then snapping Daybreaker into a gallop, she rode away from the small ranch.

She could not bring herself to look back and so did not see the lonely figure of her grandpa as he stood watching for a long while until both she and Daybreaker disappeared into the vastness of the open horizon.

It was three days later that a lone stranger came riding up to the Caillou ranch.

It was nearing dusk and the old man had just completed his meager choring duties and was strolling along the outside of the corral, watching his horses. He briefly contemplated how these once strong and vital animals had likewise lost their enthusiasm to age and now just wandered around their enclosure with a lack of purpose—and then he realized that he was just feeling sorry for himself.

The truth was that he desperately missed his granddaughter.

The deeper truth was that he feared this time she might not be coming back.

He'd tried to busy himself these past few days to keep from worrying about her. But there wasn't much he could do anymore; his physical stamina was limited due to age, injury, and advanced arthritis. He also suffered from failing eyesight from too much time in the glaring sun, though he tried his utmost to keep this from his granddaughter so that she wouldn't worry.

What little he could do was not sufficient to occupy his thoughts.

He was preparing to go inside for his supper when he saw the stranger approach from the west. He appeared as a silhouette against the bright orange glow of the setting sun, riding through the field of saguaro and bosques of mesquite. The old man cupped a hand over his eyes to lessen the glare, though all he could make out for certain was that whoever it was that was nearing the ranch was riding a large mount.

The old man scratched his forehead curiously and continued to watch as the rider advanced. He didn't know who would be coming out his way. He wasn't expecting anyone; never had any visitors, except the Mexican girl Elena whom Denim asked to come around to check up on him whenever she was away on a tour. The only other caller in recent months had been that fella who'd been keen on Denim, Jake Bradley, but he'd since moved on to California after Denim repeatedly turned down his proposals of marriage.

For a moment Grandpa thought it might be a Chiricahua scout. But he quickly dismissed that notion. While renegades under the leadership of Geronimo were still known to raid settlements throughout the Southwest, the Apache was too cunning in his strategy to prepare for an attack in so outward a manner.

The old man had lived too long on the frontier to have any fear of the approaching stranger. He walked forward to meet him.

The rider brought his mount to a halt just outside the rough-hewn fence surrounding the small acreage.

The stranger offered an amiable smile. "Hello," he announced pleasantly.

"Hullo yourself," the old man returned.

Grandpa took his first good look at the rider and wasn't sure of his impression. He was a peculiar-looking sort. Not so much in physical appearance, but in his manner of dress. He wasn't a cowboy or trail hand, that was for certain. And he even looked a might odd for a city type. He wore a dusty crooked top hat and a long gray duster that was much too oversized for his slight frame. The man apparently had poor eyesight judging by the thick wire-rim spectacles he wore, and Grandpa thought that was a shame since he didn't seem to look much older than his granddaughter . . . and beyond his odd accoutrements wasn't at all a bad looking fellow.

"Riding back from Tucson," the stranger explained in a mellow voice. "Saw your place and thought that I might rest my horse awhile."

The old man nodded. He walked through the gate toward the stranger and gave the chestnut-colored quarter horse a hearty pat. "Nice sturdy animal," he said admiringly. "Got a few of 'em myself in the corral, but surely wouldn't set 'em out on any long trail." He turned his attention back to the rider. "Sure, rest your horse for a spell. Got a trough out back if'n you'd care to feed her some water."

"Why, that's mighty obliging, sir," the stranger said appreciatively. "Think I'll take you up on your kind offer."

The old man cleared his throat. "Tucson, y'say?"

The man tipped the narrow brim of his top hat up over his forehead and wiped his brow. "A stopover from some business I had in Phoenix. I'm from up East originally. Got another stop in New Mexico, then I'll stable Dixie and be heading back."

"Kinda slow way to be travelin'," the old man remarked curiously. "Unsafe too."

"Prefer to travel that way, sir," the stranger answered politely. "The desert provides solitude that's good for a man's soul. Don't get much chance to be alone living in the big city."

The old man considered. "Reckon not. Got a granddaughter who thinks the same way. Don't necessarily agree with her . . . but you're welcome to come inside. I was just about to have some supper."

"That's mighty kind of you, sir," the stranger again said with appreciation.

The old man brushed aside his gratitude. "No need to be thankin' me," he said. "With my granddaughter away it gets mighty lonesome here. Could appreciate some company. By the way, didn't catch your name."

"It's Benjamin, sir," the stranger replied with a grin.

The old man extended his left hand, the one not as troubled by arthritis. "I'm Jason Cole, Mr. Benjamin."

"Just Benjamin," the man said, accepting the handshake.

After the horse was led to the trough and given some water and fed some oats, the two men went inside the house. At Grandpa's invitation Benjamin took a seat at the small eating table while the old man poured coffee and dished out two bowls of stew.

Taking his own chair, Grandpa broke off a chunk of bread then pushed the loaf across the table to his guest.

"Stew might be a little on the watery side," he said. "Better if you sop it up with bread. Fact is, never much learned to cook."

Benjamin smiled. "Looks just fine, Mr. Cole." He took a sip of coffee, suppressed a grimace at how strong it was, then asked casually, "You say you live her with—your daughter?"

"Granddaughter," the old man corrected. He spooned up some stew. "Yeh, just the two of us since my wife died. Laurie . . . that's my granddaughter, she's gone fer a spell. Won't be back—" He hesitated and the expression on his face became momentarily pained. "Reckon I don't rightly know." He paused again, then added with pride, "She rides with the Wild West Show. She's in Mexico now. Here, lemme show you a picture of her."

"I'd be most pleased to see it," Benjamin said.

The old man reached inside his vest to his shirt breast pocket and pulled out a gold pocket watch. He carefully handed it across to his guest.

Benjamin rotated the watch, admiring the outer casing before he clicked open the cover. The timepiece itself was impressive, the numerals inlaid in gold. But what instantly caught Benjamin's eye was the little photograph that graced the frame of the inside cover. It was a picture of a beautiful young woman—

One not unfamiliar to him.

He adjusted his spectacles and continued admiring the photograph. "Laurie, you said her name is?"

"Name she was born with. But most everyone knows her better by her show name: Denim Ryder. Y'heard of her?"

Benjamin slowly shook his head. "No," he answered quietly.

"Well, I reckon you probably wouldn't if you're not from around these parts," Grandpa muttered.

"But she's an awfully pretty girl," Benjamin stated. "You must be very proud of her, Mr. Cole."

"Got the looks of her ma," the old man said. Then, as if in afterthought, "Durn right I'm proud of her."

Benjamin finally snapped the cover closed and laid the watch on the table. He wasn't aware that his expression suddenly looked a little strange, but the old man seemed to take no notice of it.

They finished their meal mostly in silence and afterward shared more coffee while Grandpa stuffed tobacco into his pipe.

"Never smoke indoors when the girl's around," he admitted with a mischievous wink, striking a match to his boot heel and lighting the tobacco in the bowl, then puffing contentedly on the stem.

The two men conversed idly. Finally Benjamin glanced out the window. The skies had darkened to a deep blue over the purple edge of the western horizon. Charcoal smudges rolled against the late twilight backdrop.

"I guess I made myself a mite too relaxed," Benjamin

said with slight embarrassment as he started to rise from his chair.

Grandpa also rose. "Listen, young fella, why don't I fix you a place to bed down and you can leave at sunup."

Benjamin flashed a toothy smile. "Tempting offer, Mr. Cole. But you've already been mighty hospitable. Besides, lately I've kinda taken to sleeping under the stars. Got my bedroll."

"Not necessarily wise to be travelin' these parts after dark," Grandpa cautioned.

"Appreciate your concern, but I carry protection," Benjamin replied. "Actually I'm pretty handy with a gun."

The old man gave his head a shake. "Reckon I can't figger you, son. You say you're city born an' bred . . . and you sound just like my granddaughter."

"I hope that's not a bad thing," Benjamin said.

"No," the old man said. "Just not lookin' for an obligin'. City folk just never struck me as the type to turn down an invite."

"Well, sir, I did accept your invitation to a meal," Benjamin reminded pleasantly.

"Yeh, I reckon you did," the old man chuckled.

Benjamin shifted the topic. "You must worry about her when she's off by herself. Your granddaughter, I mean."

"All the time," Grandpa replied solemnly. "But what can I do 'bout it? She's got the same mule-headed stubbornness her ma had. But I'll tell you this: There ain't no girl who can take better care of herself." His voice began to trail off. "If'n she don't go off and do somethin' foolish . . ."

Benjamin extended his hand. "I thank you again for the meal, Mr. Cole. It's been a real pleasure meeting you."

The old man again met his grip with his left hand. "Offer still stands," he said.

"And I appreciate it, sir. Truly do." Benjamin lifted the gold pocket watch from the table and again snapped open the cover to admire the picture inside. "Yessir," he sighed, "she's a right fine-looking girl."

The old man spoke up. "And she'll make a fine wife someday if she ever gets it in her head to start actin' like a woman."

Benjamin continued to gaze at the picture as he started to slowly, absently, walk around the table. "He'll be an awfully lucky fella, whoever that is," he said.

"Say, young fella," Grandpa said suddenly. "May be none of my business, but what line of work are you in that brings you to travelin' so much?"

"Oh, I work for hire, Mr. Cole," Benjamin replied. "Most of my business keeps me out West."

"I hope you don't mind my askin'," Grandpa said apologetically. "But y'see, your type's rare around these parts. I notice that you don't have the hands of no cowpuncher." He quickly added: "I don't mean no insult."

Benjamin smiled oddly and snapped closed the watch. He continued to slowly circle the table.

"No offense taken," he said politely, though his smile suddenly didn't look as friendly as it had earlier. In fact, there was now something vaguely discomforting about it. "No, Mr. Cole, my work is a little more . . . specialized."

"What d'you mean by 'specialized'?" Grandpa asked, not comprehending.

"Let's just say there's a reason I don't have hands like a . . . as you say, cowpuncher."

All of a sudden, the old man felt strangely weak and he had to sit himself down at the table. The air had gotten heavy inside the little house and he was finding it difficult to breathe.

"In fact," Benjamin said, "I'd be willing to wager you've heard of me through my work."

A shadow fell over the old man's shoulder as he leaned forward on the table. Benjamin was standing directly behind him.

His voice was smooth, but becoming dark and chilling like the shadow that loomed over the old man. "Like your granddaughter, Mr. Cole, most people know me by another name. Ben . . . Ben Straker."

The old man had only a second to connect the name. A second of recognition. A second in which a thousand past previously hidden terrors came at him in a rush. A second where all the hopes, dreams, and disappointments of his life suddenly became so meaningless.

Only a second . . . before he felt the press of cold hard metal against the back of his skull.

He never heard the gunshot.

Chapter Three

The Gunslinger

Ben Straker's bloody reputation as a hired gun followed him throughout the Southwest. Yet if any man remained an anomaly to such a violent life, it was he. Refined and college educated, Benjamin Straker enjoyed a wealthy eastern upbringing replete with all the comforts and privileges. As the only son of a successful Boston importer, he was heir to the family business, which also guaranteed him acceptance into Massachusetts society. A prosperous future was seen by all for the intelligent and handsome young man.

After graduating college, Benjamin went to work for his father. Newspaper society columns soon announced his forthcoming marriage to a beautiful young debutante whose family enjoyed the same social standing as his own.

But then, after fulfilling the obligations that were

expected of him, Benjamin Straker one day walked away from his impending marriage, gave up his privileged life, and headed west.

Little was known about those years when Benjamin Straker, Esq., evolved into Ben Straker, gunman. It was said that he rode alongside Billy the Kid in New Mexico and also participated in the Lincoln County War. Ben developed a strong kinship with Bill Bonney, perhaps because of their shared eastern roots. The Kid wasn't much of a talker, but he was good at cards and he and Ben had played many a hand together. Ben displayed a natural propensity for handling a gun, which he nurtured under the tutelage of The Kid. Ben proved himself an eager and able student. In fact, Ben Straker was the only man besides Pat Garrett who was known to outdraw Billy.

Pat Garrett . . . Ben regarded Garrett's "fearless lawman" reputation with contempt. After Billy was gunned down by his former "friend," Ben concluded that Garrett had never given The Kid a fair chance. Many people sided with Ben's assertion but the coroner's jury ruled Billy's death a "justifiable homicide." Ben regarded the killing an outright act of cowardice and vowed to some day avenge Billy's murder. It was speculated that this was the reason Pat Garrett disappeared into virtual obscurity soon after his famous kill. He feared, rightly, that Ben Straker had him marked as a dead man. Although Ben had made it his code never to work his trade beyond financial gain, offering his services only to those who hired him, he welcomed the day when he and Pat Garrett might meet face-to-face.

The Kid had been dead going on two years. Just a year later Ben received more disturbing news when he learned that Jesse James had likewise been the victim of a cowardly killing. The outlaw, retired and trying to lead a peaceful life with his family, had been shot in the back by one of his own: a punk named Bob Ford, who was now enjoying the same undeserved celebrity as Pat Garrett. Ben's path had never crossed with the James gang and he felt no obligation to even the score with Bob Ford. But it did reinforce in him the desire to remain his own man—a loner in his profession.

Ben Straker was not quite twenty-seven. He was a handsome, youthful-looking man with clean features who took to presenting himself in the guise of an underfed itinerant: thick-lensed spectacles, incongruous top hat, and an ill-fitting duster flecked with trail dirt in which he handily concealed the short-barreled rifle he'd had crafted by a Reno gunsmith. It was a "specialty" which, through practice, Ben had become proficient at handling: he could produce and fire the weapon in one quick fluid movement before a draw could be made against him.

But a fair chance was rarely what Ben Straker gave his victims. When called upon to provide a service, Ben struck with the suddenness and venom of a rattlesnake—though even a rattler gives warning. There was no place for a conscience in his work, and Ben had gunned down men in full view of their families, leaving mothers, wives, and children to cry over the fallen body while he calmly rode on to his next assignment. Often even the law did not interfere, being both fearful of the man and also aware that the only people who could pay Ben Straker's high fees were those with tremendous political influence who could well afford to protect their hired gun.

The only kindness that could be said for Ben Straker was that his victims were usually dead before they even knew they had been targeted by him. It was a small mercy.

It was a blistering Saturday night in a shantytown saloon just south of Tucson. Because it was so hot, the place was filled to capacity with thirsty patrons. Ben was idly shuffling a deck of cards, sitting at a table with some of the men who worked the copper mines in Bisbee. The men were getting drunk in preparation of their visit to the various bordellos along the main strip.

Ben had removed his duster and top hat but still had on the spectacles that gave him the appearance of a Bible salesman. He listened without comment to the loud, incessant bragging of the tough miners and quietly tolerated the occasional jabs at his physical delicacy.

But his attention piqued when the conversation at the table next to him shifted to the still-celebrated killing of Billy the Kid.

"It was murder, plain and simple," one of the men insisted.

"You don't call killin' no mad dog murder," a burly, rough-edged miner named Bill Slater argued. "Pat Garrett gave The Kid the same chance The Kid gave to others. If he didn't shoot him fair, call it simple justice. The Kid deserved a bullet, however he got it. He was nothin' more than a cold-blooded punk."

"Amen," one of the men sounded.

Another sympathetic voice at the table piped up. "He hadda turn mean after Lew Wallace wouldn't go fair with him after he turned himself in."

Bill Slater spoke impatiently. "Yeh, and if *Governor* Wallace had just stuck to his duty and hanged him on the spot, a lotta good men would still be alive."

"So what is it that you're sayin', Bill?" one of his slack-jawed tablemates drawled.

Bill Slater punched the air for emphasis. "I'll tell you what I'm sayin'. That the Kid was a varmint. A murderin' little coward who got just what he deserved."

"Amen," the voice said again.

"Must make you feel like a big man to say that, Bill—'specially knowin' that The Kid ain't around to hear them words," one of the miners said, only half joking.

"If'n The Kid was here I'd tell him to his face," Bill Slater boasted. "I ain't afraid of him or no one like him."

As if to underscore his bravado he then expectorated, his stream of tobacco juice just missing the cuspidor at the side of the table.

"And that's what I think of Mr. Billy the Kid," Bill Slater concluded.

Finally Ben Straker spoke up. "You don't know what you're talking about, mister," he said calmly, still shuffling the playing cards.

Bill Slater swung his heavy-lidded eyes across to the

next table. "Well, lookee here. Now we're gonna get us a true education from this here tenderfoot," he said sardonically.

"You know his real name, dirt-choker?" Ben asked casually.

"What? Whose real name?" Bill Slater asked, too drunk to fully comprehend.

"Billy the Kid?"

"Yeah," Bill Slater ejaculated. "Sure I does. And I can spell it for you: S-K-U-N-K."

Only no one at the table laughed. It was strange yet palpable: Each of the men began to experience an uncomfortable chill that seemed to emanate from the slim, slight stranger.

Ben regarded the tough Bill Slater with a thin smile. "You're not as illiterate as you look," he said.

"Illiter—*what*?" Bill Slater demanded.

"Stupid," Ben clarified.

Bill Slater erupted. "That kinda talk I'll take from no man. But 'specially not from someone who speaks up for trash like Billy the Kid." The burly miner started to rise from his seat as the saloon quickly fell quiet. His hands impulsively closed into huge fists that he was ready to use on the stranger.

"Aw, go easy on him, Bill," one of the men at his table said, trying to ease the tension. "He's just a kid. He don't know nothin'."

"He knows enough—or thinks he does," Bill Slater

growled. He thrust a thick, oily finger at Ben. "Lissen here, you dandified little punk. I worked my whole life diggin' in the mines. Worked hard for my earnin's. I got no sympathy for no outlaws or no outlaw lover."

Ben gazed down at the cards in his hand and then gently laid them facedown on the table. He slowly removed his spectacles and then looked back up and stared narrowly at Bill Slater.

His voice remained even. "That's your problem. You've lived so long in the mud your brain's turned to rot."

Bill Slater could barely contain his fury. His ruddy face was now splotched with deep shades of crimson.

"You'd better be willin' to back up them words," he challenged.

Ben merely leaned back in his chair. He sighed. "Mighty tempting offer to rid the West of you. But there's no percentage in it."

"You gonna let him talk to you like that, Bill?" yelped a voice eager for blood.

Bill Slater withdrew his six-shooter, cocked it, and aimed the barrel straight at Ben, who didn't flinch.

The tension was thick in the saloon. No one moved. No one hardly even breathed. Everyone knew Bill Slater. He was a bully even when sober. He was completely unpredictable when drunk—and provoked. The ignorant stranger didn't seem aware that he had provided the match to a stick of dynamite.

Then, after a few moments, Ben blew out his breath and

pushed his chair back. Ignoring Bill Slater, he said to the others at his table: "It's been enlightening, boys. Hope to have the pleasure again real soon."

Bill Slater's face went even redder. "You'll be seein' me sooner'n that, you outlaw-kissin' scum."

Ben reached for his duster and top hat. He paused, then said, "Since you're so persistent, why don't we step outside. Just the two of us." He glanced around the room. "If you gentlemen don't mind affording us a little privacy."

"And I don't much care for all your fancy talk," Bill Slater added.

Ben smiled. "You like tobacco?"

"Only baccer we got's for chawin'," Bill Slater replied through yellowed teeth that stood as testimony of the fact.

Ben pulled out a gold cigarette case.

Bill Slater's eyes widened. "Genuine smokin' tobackee?" he asked.

"Premium. Imported. Come join me outside for a smoke if you have a mind to," Ben offered.

Ben walked outside the saloon and lit a cigarette. Sure enough, Bill Slater soon staggered from the swinging doors and walked toward him. His gun still dangled from his fingers.

"Just to tell you, I ain't to be forgettin' what you said in there," he instantly reminded.

Ben just nodded and led him to the shadowy dark lane at the side of the saloon. There he gave Bill Slater a cigarette and then produced a small flask of whiskey that he also handed to the miner.

"Suppose I did speak out of line," Ben said by way of an apology.

Bill Slater greedily slurped down a mouthful of the liquor. "Damn right you did. Shoulda killed you dead on the spot."

"Well, I appreciate that you didn't," Ben said gratefully.

Bill Slater took another swallow of the whiskey then handed the flask back to Ben, who said, "Go ahead. Finish it."

As Bill Slater raised his head to swallow the last remaining drops of whiskey, Ben's hand slowly disappeared inside his long coat, emerging from the underskirt brandishing a Bowie knife . . . which he quickly plunged into the miner's ample gut, though not deep enough to inflict a fatal wound.

But the pain was great and a surprised Bill Slater cried out, "You varmint! You killed me!"

Ben replied in a voice all the more chilling for its calm. "From now on keep your mouth shut about things you don't know anything about. Consider this friendly advice." Then, he gave the blade a sharp twist before withdrawing it. Bill Slater screamed in agony and dropped to his knees.

Ben removed a cloth from his pocket and wiped the blood from his knife. "There's a sawbones down the street. Have that tended to before you bleed to death."

Ben walked away without a glance back at the moaning miner, satisfied that he had both defended the name of his friend, at the same time not betraying his professional code by killing the man.

He climbed onto his horse and calmly rode out of town. He had a new destination, summoned by an urgent request. He'd received a telegram earlier that day instructing him to proceed immediately to the town of Prosperity. . . .

Chapter Four

The Town

The Wabowda Valley presented itself as a lush, alive paradise after her days on the desert.

The air was cool and clean and both she and Daybreaker felt refreshed as they rode across the sweeping grasslands under wide blue skies.

Toward noon, Denim Ryder noticed a breaking in the landscape. Off in the distance rose an outcropping of hills, the passage over which would see her into Prosperity. She began the final leg of her journey with a sense of accomplishment, though her task was just beginning.

As she crested the sloping ridge that overlooked her destination, she brought her mount to a halt and finally gave thought to what would await her once she entered the town. From her vantage point Prosperity looked to be an unassuming, peaceful place, little different from any other town that she had visited in her professional travels throughout the Southwest, built inside a valley clearing with a single dirt road bisecting the major business establishments of the town.

Denim could see that the town remained in development, with many of the wood-frame buildings unpainted and others still under construction. But she could recognize a saloon, hotel, bank, general store, barber shop, and a variety of smaller enterprises and offices whose construction had been a priority. Just beyond the outskirts of the town she could even spot the gleaming white steeple of a church. And of course, as with any town in the West, there was a jail and courthouse, both situated in the municipal building.

But Denim knew there was only one man who dispensed justice in the town of Prosperity—its boss: Brock Donovan. He was judge, jury, and if need be, executioner. Through his manipulations he could claim ownership to much of the territory extending north: rich fertile land once populated by the Apaches, parcels of which Donovan sold at high prices to families looking to settle there. Water rights on the western ridge were quickly established by monopoly, and Donovan soon became a very wealthy and powerful man.

In Prosperity, the term "fair justice" was a farce. Whatever law existed was solely at the discretion of Brock Donovan and enforced by his hand-picked committee and puppet sheriff, Tom Brough.

Prosperity prided itself on being a man's town, where

women were not recognized for the independence with which Denim Ryder would present herself. Although men drank and gambled freely along the main strip, their wives and daughters were expected to behave in a proper ladylike fashion—in both manner and attire. In fact, it was understood that the only times a woman was allowed into town unescorted were on Saturday afternoons for shopping and Sunday mornings for worship. It was a rule established by Brock Donovan, since the town also employed a stable of "ladies of questional repute" whom he allowed to freely ply their trade among "respectable" and married gentlemen.

This was the town where Denim Ryder had come seeking a man. One whom she intended to kill. The most feared and respected man in the territory. Brock Donovan.

She waited until dusk before she rode into town. She tried to remember what day it was, and settled on Friday. She took the main street toward the false-fronted saloon, her hand tight on the pommel of the saddle. She set herself free from the apprehension that had begun to gnaw at her insides, bracing herself with a confidence borne of lifelong independence and now a singular purpose. She lifted herself down from her horse and looped the reins around the hitching rail in front of the saloon. She removed her gloves and rubbed the palms of her hands along her long, shapely legs, snug inside a pair of tight blue jeans, over which she wore leather chaps. The denim fabric was sun-faded and the well-worn material now felt almost like velvet against her skin. Her denim shirt and open leather vest were dusty from the trail and she gave both a quick brush with her hands. She loosened the drawstring under her chin but did not remove her Stetson. Although there could be no mistaking her gender, she still swept her long blond hair up under her hat. And then she prepared herself for the reception she knew awaited her in the male-dominated town of Prosperity.

An unwashed, unshaven cowboy, himself apparently just off the trail, dressed in battered brown trousers and a blue plaid shirt, with a bandanna tied around his neck, stood leaning against the front of the saloon, rolling a cigarette and squinting against the setting sun. Denim made herself look him straight in the eye as she passed, anticipating and ready for her first confrontation, but the cowboy merely regarded her with quiet indifference.

Denim's boots and jangling spurs sounded against the raised heavy planking as she strode past him into the saloon.

It was called the Golden Circle Saloon, and despite its colorful name it was an establishment that Denim immediately found gloomy and cheerless, lacking any atmosphere of color or gaiety. But then she'd never been inside a saloon before to give it a fair comparison. As she walked toward the bar, Denim studied the place. A heavy wagon-wheel chandelier hung from the center of the ceiling. There were about a dozen circular tables scattered about, an old upright player piano braced against the far wall, and, of course, the brass-railed serving counter that stretched the length of the back wall. A semi-ornate backbar was set behind the counter, built around a large mirror and flanked by bottles of assorted liquor. At the left of the bar was a staircase leading to the second-floor balcony, which apparently provided rooming accomodations. Only a few gaudy decorations graced the walls: a mounted longhorn head, a display of various tools connected with the cattle trade, and three dusty oil paintings, each show-casing a hefty barroom nude in poses quite suggestive for the time.

In short, it was a place that did not invite female pa-tronage.

Eyes had shifted toward the girl as she entered the saloon and a sudden hush fell over the room. The place was half-filled with cowboys and local ranchers, a hard-looking bunch, and not one returned to his drinking or card playing. Each man remained curiously focused on this intriguing female stranger who clearly was not wise to the ways of Prosperity.

Denim ignored their stares and walked straight up to the bar. At first the barkeep paid her no attention, though she caught him casting furtive glances at his customers to gauge their reactions.

Finally Denim said: "I'll be needin' a room . . . and a bath."

The barkeep, Joe McDonald, was a big-bellied man, fat as a hog, for whom even the simple act of drawing a breath seemed an exertion. He had a thick, beet-red face that even in repose registered a fierce expression.

He shook his sweaty, balding head and said in a gravelly

voice: “We don’t serve no women here. ’Specially no girly women.”

A roar of laughter erupted in the saloon.

Denim slowly turned to look at the tables. “I say somethin’ funny?” she said.

The men quieted but continued to regard her with amusement.

“You got a real spitfire here, Joe,” a grizzled old cowboy cackled.

“Ain’t what you said,” Joe McDonald gruffly explained to the girl. “It’s what you done.”

“And what’s that?” Denim asked.

Joe heaved a wheezy breath. “Put simple, little miss, womenfolk ain’t allowed into town unescorted. And outside of our entertainment and servin’ girls, ain’t one allowed to step foot inside this saloon.”

“*Allowed?*” Denim echoed curiously, narrowing her eyes.

“Them’s the rules,” Joe said as he started wiping beer stains from the counter with a dirty cloth.

Denim spoke up boldly. “Mr. Donovan’s rules?”

Joe ignored her question as he observed the girl’s gun belt.

“I’d advise you not to be packin’ side arms,” he said.

“And I’d be tellin’ you that I don’t make it *my* rule not be be ridin’ into a strange town without protectin’ myself,” Denim returned insolently.

Joe fell silent, though he maintained his unpleasant expression.

"How d'you know that's what she is, Joe?" a man named Charlie Pratt shouted from another table. "A woman, I mean. Never knowed no fee-male to dress like a pistol-packin' trail duster."

Denim paid him no attention and again said to the bar-keep: "I was askin' you if my not bein' welcome here is Donovan's rule."

Again the men burst into boisterous laughter. The girl was sure full of spunk—if not much sense.

Joe drew a beer on tap for a customer who'd signaled him. "*Mister* Donovan," he corrected, with proper emphasis.

The corners of Denim's full lips curved up in an ironic smile. "Well, just that you should be knowin', your *Mister* Donovan is just the man I come to town to see."

"And what dealin's would you be havin' with Mr. Donovan?" Joe inquired, his lips curled in a smirk, as amused by the idea as he was curious.

Denim was tired to the point of orneriness, but she kept her temper in check and ignored his question. "It's almost nightfall and I've come a long way," she said. "I'd 'preciate gettin' that room."

Joe was blunt. "Can't oblige you."

Now Denim started to get impatient. "Then can you tell me just where I can get a place for the night?"

Then—she heard the distinct sound of a woman coughing. She took a step back from the bar and let her eyes wander around the saloon. Nestled in a corner next to the player piano, seated at a table for two, was a woman holding a shot glass and, most curious to Denim, smoking a slim cigar.

Denim turned back to the barkeep. "I thought you said ladies wasn't allowed in town," she remarked, giving her head a nudge in the woman's direction.

"That ain't no lady. That's Marie!" interjected Charlie Pratt.

The men all whooped in agreement.

"Okay, quiet down, all of you," Joe ordered firmly. To Denim he said: "Marie works here. Singer . . . or used to be. Now she watches over the servin' girls."

Denim looked askance at the auburn-haired middle-aged woman and gave her a quick appraisal. She'd never seen a real saloon girl before and, truthfully, wasn't much impressed. She could tell instantly that Marie had a tough attitude, and the way she was dressed in her fancy, frilly garments suggested to Denim that maybe at one time she *had* been in show business.

Joe again spoke with a blunt edge. "Like you said, gonna be dark soon. I'd advise you to be ridin' out."

"You still didn't answer my question," Denim said sharply.

"Ain't no place in town for you," Joe repeated sternly.

"Joe, you've got the face of a pig and could only hope to have the manners of one."

It was Marie talking, in a slightly accented, tobacco-tarnished voice. She got up from her table carrying her shot glass and walked over to the bar.

She studied the girl cowboy before fixing her with a tight smile. "I'll see that you get a room, honey. But down the street at the hotel. I wouldn't insult you by letting you spend the night in this . . . rustler's purgatory."

The woman was slightly inebriated; Denim could smell the gin wafting off her breath. But she was grateful for the woman's offer.

"Now you hold on a minute, Marie," Joe McDonald protested. "You know Mr. Donovan's got a strict policy 'bout—"

"You let me worry about Mr. Donovan's 'policy,' " Marie replied abruptly.

"Yeh, and she's 'bout the only one that can!" Charlie Pratt chortled, his comment producing raucous laughter from his companions.

Marie turned stiffly toward him and said in a straight voice: "Charlie, why don't you finish that bottle and take a quick tumble off your horse."

"That's tellin' him, Marie!" one of his cronies applauded.

Marie refocused her attention on Denim. She poured a splash of gin from the bottle on the counter into her shot glass.

She looked carefully at the girl and said: "I'd offer you a drink, honey, but you don't look old enough to even be in a place like this."

"I'm twenty-two," Denim replied. "But I don't take to liquor."

"Smart girl." Marie winked at her and raised her shot glass in a salute before downing it. She grimaced as the strong alcohol burned its way down her throat, then added: "Twenty-two?" Her face looked a little sad. "I wouldn't have guessed," she said in a subdued tone.

Denim took a quick study of Marie and pondered how this woman had the potential to reach her middle years with an attractive grace. Instead, her face was lined and hard and she looked much older than what likely were her calendar years.

Marie started to pour yet another shot when she suddenly erupted into a prolonged coughing spasm. Denim spun around to Joe McDonald, who appeared unconcerned as he towel-wiped glasses behind the bar.

"Ain't you gonna do somethin'?" Denim said urgently.

Joe just shrugged. "Happens all the time. She'll cough her way outta it."

Gradually Marie recovered, though the attack had left her pale and short of breath. Denim helped her back to her table.

"You want I should get some water or somethin'?" she asked with concern.

Marie waited a few moments to regain her breath. She shook her head and said hoarsely: "No. Like Joe says, happens all the time."

Joe poured another shot of gin, which he brought over to her table.

"That ain't no healthy-soundin' cough," Denim said. "Maybe you should be seein' a doctor."

Marie smiled. "Just allergies," she replied dismissively.

She then inhaled and slowly exhaled. "Guess I've never quite grown accustomed to the desert."

"You ain't from around these parts?" Denim inquired politely.

Marie was still a little short of air. She glanced up at Denim, who was standing opposite her, leaning forward across the table, and she sort of scolded her. "When I speak to someone I prefer to talk to 'em straight in the eye. So pull up a chair and sit down."

Denim smiled demurely and slid out the chair from the other side of the small table. She spun it around so that its back faced the table and then plopped herself wide-legged on the seat. She leaned forward and clasped her hands across the raised back of the chair. Marie could not help smiling to herself. If this girl possessed any feminine delicacy beyond her natural beauty, she wasn't quick to display it.

"No," Marie finally said in answer to her question. "Actually I'm from Canada. A place called Quebec."

"Canada!" Denim exclaimed, reacting as if Marie had said she'd come from another planet. "How in tarnations did you ever end up here?"

"That's a story for another day," Marie said simply.

"That's heavy snow country, ain't it?" Denim asked with interest.

Marie nodded. "About as far as you can get from the weather here. Now suppose you tell me about yourself?"

Denim looked uncertain. "Ain't much to tell."

"Well—you must come from someplace," Marie prodded.

Denim scratched the nape of her neck. "Yeh. South of here. Place you probably never heard of. Caillou. It's a small territory named after my grandpa's ranch. But I didn't come from there. Fact is, just rode in from Mexico."

"You *rode* in. By yourself?" Marie was intrigued.

"Yes'm," Denim said proudly.

"That's a long journey," Marie remarked.

Denim widened her eyes. "Longer'n expected. Desert trail. Hot days. High winds. Even rode into a sandstorm. Weren't sure if we'd make it."

Marie looked puzzled. "*We*? I thought you said you rode in alone?"

"By *we*, I mean me and my horse, Daybreaker," Denim explained with a radiant grin that instantly accentuated the dimples in her cheeks.

"You didn't have to come by way of the Tellahu," Marie said curiously.

"I know that. Thought it would be quicker. And . . . I kinda liked the challenge. Misjudged on a few things, though." Denim looked a bit embarrassed at this admission.

Marie just gave her head a shake. Then her voice assumed a probing tone. "Quite a ride just to see Brock Donovan. Must be pretty important."

Denim shifted uncomfortably. "Ma'am . . ."

"The name's Marie. Marie DuBois," she corrected. "Let's keep it friendly between us." For the first time Marie offered a genuinely warm smile, which Denim had already determined was a rare expression for her.

Denim smiled back but fumbled with what she was trying to say. "I'd like that fine, ma'am—uh, Marie. But y'see, and I don't mean to sound rude, but my business with Brock Donovan is kinda personal."

Marie studied the girl for a moment, her curiosity piqued. But she obliged by changing the subject. "You look like you could use a good meal."

Denim brightened. "Well, yes, ma'am. Ain't been eatin' much more than biscuits and berries these past days. And a little jerky—but careful like 'cause of the salt."

"We'll go down to the hotel and get you a room," Marie offered. She then looked over at Joe McDonald, who was watching them. She spoke in a deliberate voice: "And a meal you can digest, not one that's still bucking on the plate."

"Aww, Marie, you know we get serviced by the hotel," Joe said.

"Yeah, but it's what you do to it once it gets here that keeps Doc Brennan busy," Marie retorted.

Denim brushed back under the Stetson the stringy strands of hair that had fallen out over the sides of her face. She said: "Seems kinda funny you wantin' to help me and all an' I ain't even told you my name."

"You do have me at a disadvantage," Marie acknowledged.

Denim extended her arm ramrod-straight across the table.

"Name's Laurette. But I prefer Laurie. Most everyone calls me Denim, though."

Marie's hand met the girl's and she was surprised at the strength and firmness of her grip.

"Denim," she mused.

"My grandpa started callin' me that," Denim explained with another dimple-enhancing grin. " 'Cause of the way I dress."

Marie smiled agreeably. "Makes sense. And you say you were just in Mexico?"

"On Sam Abbott's show circuit. Up 'til 'bout a week ago."

Marie was interested. "Performer?"

Denim shrugged modestly. "Do some shootin' and ridin'. Speakin' of which, Daybreaker, my horse, is every bit as tired as I am. Sure would like to get him stabled and fed."

"Livery stable's just down the street," Marie told her. "Why don't we get you settled and I'll harness one of these courteous gentlemen to attend to your horse."

"Oh no, ma'am—uh, Marie," Denim said quickly. "Daybreaker don't take to no one but me. We been through so much together, he just don't trust no one else."

Marie looked at the girl. "All right. Let's get that taken care of first and then get you fed."

"Sounds fine, ma'am," Denim said appreciatively. And she got up from the chair.

"Marie," the woman corrected again. "By the way," she added, glancing across at one of the cowboys, all of whom by now had returned to their card playing or imbibing.

"Don't pay no mind to anything Charlie Pratt there says. He's not known around these parts as Stinkweed for nothing."

"I ain't." Denim smiled. Then she registered a curious expression and wrinkled her nose. "Though that reminds me . . . I could sure use a bath."

Marie wasn't about to disagree. "Amen to that, child."

Chapter Five

The Cowboy

George Merrell was a farmer, plain and simple. He'd worked his small acreage for going on four years and managed to eke out a living from his livestock ranching. George lived with the knowledge that he could have been more successful if he had gone along with the other farmers in the valley and joined the market association headed by Brock Donovan. His neighbors were earning good wages under this arrangement. But George had no regrets. Donovan was one man he preferred not to have any dealings with.

George worked his land with a colored man named Luther Grace. Luther never offered much about his background and George wasn't the type to question. About the only thing George did know was that Luther was a man who accepted servitude as his way in life.

During a year when George's farming earned him a little extra money, he'd traveled up to Mississippi where he found himself on a winning streak in a card game with a gentleman gambler. Desperate to recoup some of his losses, this "gentleman" offered to wager his manservant on a final draw. It was obvious that he regarded his servant as just another possession.

"I don't take to wagerin' human beings," George had said, barely concealing his disgust at the proposition.

"You ain't wagerin' him, suh," his opponent reminded haughtily. "*I* am."

Realizing that a lucky hand could set free the unappreciated servant, George accepted the offer and he played his hand—winning with a jack over a 10 high. The gambler grumbled but honored his bet, and from that moment on George referred to Luther Grace as "Lucky," a name which his new friend accepted with pride.

George never considered Lucky his property. It was Luther himself who offered to ride back with George and go to work for him. While life's circumstances had fostered in George a wary cynicism toward most people, he soon recognized in Luther a deep compassion and loyalty. He was a man on whom George knew he could depend. Almost immediately George began treating him like family, insisting that Luther did not work *for* him, but rather *with* him, allowing him to share his small house. And while both were quiet men, George enjoyed his companionship.

George Merrell was thirty-five years old. He was good-looking in a rugged sort of way, the years of hard outdoor work mapped deep into tanned, chiseled features. He had a full head of sandy hair, which was usually unkempt and long enough to curl up over the collar of his shirt. His physique was long and lean, his muscles rock hard from his labor.

George had never married because he knew he could never provide much of a life for a woman. Although he worked from sunup to dusk, he had little to show for it. A small, weathered wood-frame house and a barn always in need of repair. He was looked upon as a virtual recluse who made only occasional trips into town to pick up supplies. Most of the people who lived in the valley, including former friends, now avoided or ridiculed him as he rode by with Luther in his rickety old buckboard—because of his defiance of Brock Donovan.

But he was left pretty much alone. On occasion, after a good Saturday night drink, Donovan's ranch hands would ride out to George's farm aiming to provoke a fight. George and Luther would sit side-by-side on the porch with their rifles across their knees, calmly ignoring the threats and taunts until the drunken troublemakers would gallop off in frustration.

George was a strong man, and no coward. But he chose to live his life peacefully and avoided trouble wherever possible.

George Merrell was the cowboy Denim had seen standing outside the Golden Circle Saloon earlier that evening.

As she and Marie were getting ready to leave for the stable George came inside the saloon and at Marie's invitation sauntered over to them.

He tipped the brim of his battered Stetson. "Evenin', ladies." He then spoke to Denim. "Spotted that handsome Winchester inside your saddle boot. If you don't mind some advice, best not to leave it open to display in this town."

Before Denim could respond there was an angry slap of cards against one of the back tables. One of the players, a hot-tempered Donovan ranch hand and ramrodder named Ned Randolph, a man with a particular dislike for George, had taken quick offense at what he perceived as an insult. He'd long been waiting for such an opportunity. "You callin' us thieves, pig farmer?" he demanded to know.

George remained calm. "Ain't speakin' 'bout no one in particular, Ned," he replied without turning to look at the man. "Just offerin' the lady here some advice."

Ned Randolph pulled himself from his chair. "I don't hear no one askin' for your advice."

"Ladies," George said to Denim and Marie as he walked over to the bar.

Marie tilted her head toward the girl. Her voice was calm. "Denim, take your horse to the livery stable and I'll catch up with you at the hotel."

"There gonna be trouble?" Denim asked with a tinge of excitement in her voice.

"None that George can't handle, if he has a mind to,"

Marie replied. Then she added under her breath: "Only he won't." She looked squarely at the girl. "Trust me, it's better if you get yourself out of here. Now go on."

Marie was shooing her off as if she were some troublesome schoolgirl, and Denim didn't much care for that. But it wouldn't serve her purpose to argue with Marie, especially since this was none of her affair, and so she did as she was told. She began to walk slowly to the swinging batwings of the saloon, stopping to take a quick look back over her shoulder.

Ned Randolph had assumed an aggressive stance: legs spread apart, right arm akimbo as if ready to draw his side arm. It wasn't a mere threat. With Brock Donovan the justice in town, shooting down George Merrell, whom Donovan likewise hated, would have no consequence for Ned Randolph. In fact, it might even earn him a cash bonus from his boss.

"Don't turn your back on me when I'm talkin' to you," Ned spat. "I'm wantin' you to explain what you said."

George lifted his foot and rested it on the brass footrail. "Gimme a shot of whiskey, Joe," he said to the burly barkeep.

Joe opened a bottle of Irish whiskey and poured George a drink, carefully keeping an eye on Ned Randolph. He didn't care who took a shot at who, but not in his establishment.

"You ain't got the guts to draw on me, is that it, pig man?" Ned said through gritted teeth.

George calmly picked up his shot glass and looked

thoughtfully into the clear amber liquid. "Don't see no percentage in it," he finally said to his antagonist, with his back still facing him. "Just leave the bottle, Joe."

After a few tense moments Ned Randolph relaxed his pose.

"Aww, this place stinks yella," he grumbled, sliding back into his chair.

Denim was still standing by the batwings, intrigued. She looked over to Marie, who gestured for her to take her horse to the livery stable. She then raised her index finger to indicate that she would join her shortly.

George poured himself another straight shot that he quickly downed.

"Ain't seen you in town for a spell," Joe said to him. "Where's your helper?"

"At the farm," George answered cordially. "And I been around, Joe, only I ain't been so noisy 'bout it."

"Smart way to be, Merrell," Joe said with a wheezing breath. "You'd do best to get done whatever business you got then skee-daddle back to that dirt farm of yours."

George slowly raised his eyes to the fat man. "I thought I might like a drink first," he said.

"In that case, maybe you might prefer some company," Marie suggested as she edged over next to him.

George ignored her presence and poured himself another shot. He wasn't much of a drinker and could already feel the effects of the whiskey.

Joe spoke up. "Ain't polite not to answer when a lady's talkin' to you."

George twisted the shot glass in his hand. "Tell you what, Joe. Find me a lady and maybe I'll work on improvin' my manners."

Joe's fat features grew even more unpleasant. He looked as though he were getting ready to physically throw George from the saloon. But Marie spoke up to defend him.

"It's okay, Joe. George didn't mean anything by it," she said pleasantly.

" 'Course not," George replied, his eyes glued on the shot glass. "I just wanta be finishin' my drink quiet."

Marie said: "If you don't want to be sociable, you could at least buy me a drink."

Ned Randolph spoke up from his table. "And pay with what? A bucket of pig slop?"

His comment generated laughter from his companions.

George did not bother to respond. But Marie did.

She glared at him from the bar and said: "And whatever we don't feed you, you can take a bath in, Ned."

Ned's face went red mean and he shot up from the table. "Maybe that pig farmer ain't no real man, but I am. And no saloon trollop's gonna—"

Joe McDonald interrupted Ned's rant by thumping his double-barreled shotgun down onto the counter. It was his "peacekeeper," which all his customers knew he kept cleaned and loaded—and out of sight behind the bar until trouble brewed.

"Ned, either you sit yourself back down or I'm gonna be scrubbin' my floor with chlorine," Joe warned.

The rage continued to build inside Ned as he stood his ground, humiliated, made to look like a jackass in the eyes of his companions, who knew him as a man not quick to back down from a fight. Women were held in low esteem in Prosperity, and to be insulted by a wise-mouthed saloon spit like Marie was almost more than Ned Randolph could tolerate.

But he had no desire to be blasted in two by a double load of buckshot, so instead he spun around on his heels and stormed out of the saloon, almost ripping the batwings from their hinges.

George never so much as glanced back.

"Merrell, even without aimin' to, you can't help causin' trouble," Joe said humorlessly as he returned the shotgun to its place under the corner.

Without meeting her eyes, George said to Marie: "What'll you have?"

"I know what she drinks," Joe cut in. He grabbed the half-consumed bottle of gin from the counter and took out a clean shot glass.

"No, Joe. Give me a real drink," Marie instructed, indicating the tall glasses neatly stacked on the shelf of the backbar.

Joe shrugged and obliged.

"And Joe . . . I'll take a fresh cigar," Marie said.

Joe reached behind the bar and withdrew one of her special blends.

"Got a light?" Marie asked George.

The cowboy flicked a match against his boot heel, but before he could light her cigar Marie broke into another harsh coughing fit.

"Fourth time today," Joe said easily, as if keeping count.

George sighed and took Marie by the shoulders and gently guided her to a nearby table.

Once she recovered George said to her: "Smokin' ceegars in your condition. I never knew anyone with such an urge to kill themself."

"Nice to know that someone gives a damn," Marie said with no emotion.

"I care for the welfare of any livin' creature," George remarked. " 'Course there're some better off just bein' put outta their misery."

"Sit with me, George," Marie asked, as a favor.

George hesitated. Then he went to the bar to retrieve his bottle. He walked back to the table and kicked out the chair across from Marie.

"I've always been nice to you," Marie said.

"Ain't sayin' you haven't," George replied. He threw back a shot of whiskey, and then his voice grew strong. Perhaps too strong. "You had a lot goin' for you, Marie."

"Referring to my illustrious stage career," she said with an ironic edge.

"Yeh. An actress. That's what you was aimin' to be," George remembered with a nod of his head.

Marie lowered her eyes. "I gave up that dream a long time ago."

George poured himself more whiskey, sloshing most over the edge of the glass and onto the table. His eyes were becoming heavy-lidded. The liquor was hitting him pretty hard. He prudently pushed the bottle aside.

Marie felt no such restraint and continued to drink straight gin from her tall glass.

"Coulda been yours, Marie," George said with a sort of regret. "But instead you rode into Prosperity and fell under the spell of Brock Donovan."

"You were working for him too, as I recall," Marie reminded.

George responded with a slow nod. "A mistake it didn't take me long to recognize," he said pensively.

Marie's tone became defensive. "Well, Brock's never done anything to me."

"Or *for* you," George was quick to add. Normally a taciturn man, the liquor was loosening his tongue. "But he made you promises. Promises like he's made everyone in the valley. He was gonna build you a big theater, put you on the stage, You'll be long dead 'fore that ever comes to be. What no one but me realizes is that the only person Brock Donovan has an interest in is *Brock Donovan*. He don't do nothin' for nobody 'less he can gain by it."

"And what about *you*, George Merrell?" Marie challenged impatiently. "Where could have you been today if you hadn't been so mule-headed stubborn? You've made yourself a joke around these parts. Everyone's making money through the association, except for you. You can't tell me Brock hasn't done a lot for these people. Giving them land so they can settle and build a decent life for themselves."

"And when it comes time to be payin' up on that debt, you can be sure he'll collect," George said, lifting his glass.

Marie smirked. "From everyone but you."

"I won't be kowtowin' to Donovan," George said straightly. "I'll keep on the way I'm goin' and least hold on to my pride. That's all a man can hope for."

"What about respect?" Marie argued, her alcohol-fueled voice raising in pitch. "You think that because you've got your pride people look at you any different? I can tell you, George Merrell, they don't."

George's bleary eyes set firmly on Marie. "But I don't come cheap," he said flatly.

It made no difference that George was speaking through his liquor. Marie reacted to the insult by grabbing his bottle of whiskey and splashing it across his face.

"Worse men than you've never said that to me," she said indignantly.

George sat motionlessly as the whiskey sluiced down his cheeks and chin. "And ain't no better man than me ever rode into Prosperity," he stated simply, wiping the liquor off his face with the back of his hand.

Joe McDonald thudded over to their table.

"Just gimme the word, Marie, and I'll throw him outta here," he said as he locked his heavy fists together and cracked his knuckles for emphasis.

George smiled at him. "Don't work yourself into a sweat,

Joe. I got what I came here for. I'm sufficiently drunk." He tossed a piece of silver across the table to Marie. "Get yourself another drink."

George pulled himself up from the chair and staggered away from the table. Marie and Joe watched him as he elbow-pushed his way through the batwings.

"One of these times he's gonna ride into town and not be ridin' out," Joe remarked.

Marie sighed. "Just another uneventful afternoon in Prosperity," she said wryly.

Chapter Six

The Boss

Marie met Denim as the blue jean–clad girl was walking along the boardwalk toward the hotel from the livery stable. Denim immediately wanted to know if there had been any trouble in the saloon, and Marie simply replied that whenever George Merrell came into town there was sure to be trouble.

She explained: "George doesn't go looking for trouble, but it always seems to follow him." She added ruefully: "In his own way, he's a dangerous man. Mostly to himself."

As they entered the lobby of the Prosperity Hotel, Denim was again curious about the reception she would get when she registered for a room. That had never been a problem when she toured with Sam Abbott, but they'd never gone into a town like Prosperity. She asked Marie where she and the other saloon girls lived. Marie explained that the girls lodged together at a boardinghouse down the street while she had her own room above the saloon. Denim was naive enough to believe the sole purpose of the girls who worked at the saloon was to serve drinks.

The desk clerk regarded Denim with the glare of suspicion that she had expected, and it was only on Marie's insistence that he reluctantly allowed her a room. Denim thought it odd that for a town boasting such male dominance everyone seemed accommodating to Marie DuBois.

After she settled in, Denim went downstairs to the hotel restaurant. She welcomed Marie's company while she enjoyed a fine meal of corn bread, beefsteak, potatoes, and greens, so tasty that she disregarded proper table manners, oblivious to the occasional disapproving glances of the other diners. Marie herself was more amused than embarrassed. Denim ate her fill and passed on dessert. She paid her bill by digging the money out of a little purse she carried around her neck.

Following dinner, she and Marie returned to her room where she luxuriated in the warm, soapy water of a bath.

"I forgot how good a bath could feel," she purred to Marie.

Marie went into the next room where she inspected the girl's clothing. "We'll have to send these out to be cleaned. Looks like you carried back half of the Tellahu with you. You brought along a change of clothes?"

"No, ma'am," Denim replied promptly. "That's purty much all I got with me, 'ceptin' for a change of undergarments."

"Glad to hear that," Marie muttered to herself. She stepped toward the open door. "You wear these when you're performing?" she asked.

"Oh no," Denim replied. "All my show outfits are provided for. For my travelin' all I need's what I got on my back. Y'see, I don't stop at no hotels when I'm ridin' back to the ranch. I like to camp out with my horse nearby, so don't need to worry 'bout changin' clothes all that much. Plus I like to travel light."

Marie breathed out a protracted sigh. "Well . . . until we get your clothes cleaned—if they don't fall apart, I mean—I'm sure I've got something I can fix you up in."

Denim spoke quickly. "None of 'em frilly dresses. Don't mean no offense, but they ain't at all to my likin'."

Marie looked bewildered. "Don't you like to pretty up once in a while?" she asked.

Denim gave her head a slight jerk and said almost shyly: "Well, ma'am, I always thought I was sorta purty without fussin' with fancy getups."

Marie smiled, and it wasn't the hard, jaded smile she'd come to adopt. Rather, it was a natural parting of the lips that revealed the softness of the innocent girl she had once been. Much like her new friend.

"You are, Denim," she said admiringly. "You're a very pretty girl."

Denim smiled brightly. "Thank you, ma'am."

"But think how much more like a lady you'd feel if you wore the right clothes."

"Don't make no difference to me," Denim said matter-of-factly. "I like bein' who I am."

Marie sighed and did not press the matter. She could see that Denim was a girl of her own mind and that it was pointless to try to change her ways.

"Well, I'll fetch you some bedclothes and have these cleaned for you tomorrow. But Denim—these jeans, they're close to being worn through."

Denim was unconcerned. "Yes, ma'am. But that's how I like 'em. Soft an' comfortable—though sometimes they're a mite uncomfortable for ridin'."

Marie planted her fists on her hips. "Denim, in all my years I swear I've never met anyone quite like you."

"Ma'am?" Denim said.

Marie nodded.

"Thing is," she said sheepishly, "I'll need them clothes early tomorrow. I'll be goin' out in the mornin'."

Marie shook her head. "I won't be able to get them ready by then. The Chinaman who does the laundry has closed up shop by now." She paused, then added: "I suppose I could wash them myself."

Denim objected. "Oh no, I couldn't ask you to do that."

Marie shushed her. "I can take them down the street. You'll have them by the time you get up. Maybe I don't look the type, but I'm not exactly a stranger to washing chores."

Denim's eyes took on a curious expression. She spoke her words carefully. "Ma'am—uh, Marie, I keep forgettin' . . . maybe it ain't right for me to be askin', but why're you takin' such a carin' of me?"

"Is that important?" Marie said.

Denim hesitated before replying. "No, I—I guess not. I just ain't used to bein' pampered. Even on the show circuit I'm purty much left to fend for myself. I kinda made it my way and people just let me be."

"Everyone needs a little looking after sometimes," Marie offered gently.

Denim looked pensive. "Reckon so. And I know it ain't a bad thing. Only it ain't somethin' I ever been used to. Even my grandpa purty much lets me to myself."

"Why don't you finish up your bath and get into bed," Marie suggested. "I'll wager you've also forgot how a soft mattress feels."

"You'd win that bet," Denim said cheerfully.

Even though it had been nearly a week since she had enjoyed the warm comfort of a bed, Denim had a difficult time falling asleep. Thoughts tumbled around in her head throughout the night and she tossed and turned in restless acknowledgment. What played out most in her brain was the realization that tomorrow she would be riding out to Brock Donovan's ranch—to confront a man she'd heard about all her life, but had never met. A man she knew only by his fearsome reputation. A reputation built on thievery, deceit—and murder.

Brock Donovan owned a large spread comfortably nestled in the heart of the Wabowda Valley. Shortly after acquiring this prime stretch of grazing land from the Apaches, Donovan went to work establishing one of the largest and most successful cattle ranches in the Southwest. Here he raised shorthorns, Durhams, and Herefords—along with an impressive stable of thoroughbred horses. To his neighbors in the valley and to others throughout the territory, Brock Donovan represented prosperity and respectability. Yet only a thorn scratch beneath the surface lay the darker truth. The green lushness of his property was as much a mirage as any come upon in the desert. For the truth was that the land upon which his herds grazed was stained red with the blood of the many people he had betrayed.

Brock Donovan had achieved the success he believed was his due in life, and he was determined to keep buried the secrets of his past. His outward appearance was an important factor in how he maintained his image. From a brutish former cowhand he had evolved into a gentleman rancher. He always dressed in the finest clothes, tailor-made affairs, and that was how he presented himself, whether he was supervising work on the range or socializing for business or pleasure. No one in the valley wore better or more expensive suits and coats than he—a show of his "gentlemanly attributes." He prided himself as a man of culture and refinement, concealing beneath the fine fabrics the true nature of the beast. But a studied look at Donovan revealed a man corrupted by greed and ruthless ambition. He was forty-nine years of age, but looked older—not so much through the natural process of aging, but because his face betrayed the blackness of his heart. He was a big man physically, inches over six feet and well over two hundred pounds. While it showed that once he could have been a handsome man, now he was possessed of thick, cruel features given to shifting expressions of benignity or ferocity, whichever the situation warranted, and eyes that were once brown but had become black and soulless, like pits leading to damnation. When he spoke, he uttered his words like a command. He focused directly on whomever he was talking to, and this often created an unsettling situation, for it was difficult for one to return a gaze into that cold, merciless stare.

That was what Donovan's ranch foreman, Roy Shannon, was experiencing as he spoke his concerns to his boss early the next morning while Donovan was having his breakfast on the veranda.

"I been tellin' you for a year that you gotta start thinkin' 'bout movin' your herds north," Roy was arguing. "The range is overgrazed and overtrampled. You're losin' ten to twelve head a week on average and that number's gonna get higher come month's end."

Donovan just stared at him over his coffee cup, his expression flat and unblinking.

Roy was quick to avert his eyes from that steady, penetrating gaze. Donovan noticed him look away, and it quietly pleased him.

"Look, Mr. Donovan," Roy went on, "you hired me to manage your cattle. I'm just statin' the facts. If you don't seriously consider movin' the herds, your only other option's gonna be to up your price. In which case your customers'll start buyin' their beef from outside the association. Your partners won't stand for it, Mr. Donovan. You gotta see clear to the economics of this thing."

Finally Donovan spoke. His words were blunt, his tone a trifle condescending. "You let me worry 'bout the economics, Mr. Shannon. And my 'partners,' as you so generously refer to 'em, they'll go along with whatever I tell 'em. You seem to be forgettin' some facts, Roy." He leaned forward in his chair for emphasis. "Who was it that set up the association? Whose money covered all the start-up costs, and who extended credit to more than a few of the members? Before I offered 'em the chance to come in on this deal, they were homesteaders froze out by the cold and grateful for the opportunity I gave 'em. Each of those men is providin' good lives for their families because of me. Be a right shame to think I no longer had their gratitude."

At that moment a young ranch worker named Cory Graham whipped his horse up to the front of the house and stopped short in a show-off display of his horsemanship.

"Y'got a visitor ridin' up, Mr. Donovan," Cory said excitedly.

Donovan furrowed his heavy brow. "I ain't expectin' no visitor," he said, displeased.

"Well, you might be wantin' to see this one," Cory said briskly, grinning and with a glint of mischief in his eyes. "Think it's a female."

"Think?" Donovan said curtly. "You been out on the range too long, boy?"

Cory lifted a shoulder. "Well, sure ain't dressed like one."

"Okay, Cory, thanks," Donovan said as a dismissal.

The young man whooped and spurred his horse into a gallop, riding back to his work post with reckless abandon.

"Damn fool kid's gonna kill himself one of these days," Roy Shannon muttered, though not with any degree of concern.

Donovan eased his bulk away from the breakfast table and slapped a heavy hand on Roy's shoulder. "I'd better greet my company. You git back to work and don't be forgettin' what I told you. Just leave everything to me." He smiled amiably, but there was no warmth in his expression. "You don't think I got to where I am by not knowin' how to play my cards right."

Denim kept Daybreaker at a steady trot as she rode the stone-bordered pathway past the widespread flower garden up toward the main house. What greeted her was unlike any ranch she had ever seen. It was more like a kind of palace than a country dwelling. Expansive, of European design, stone masonry, its gleaming white exterior and large front windows reflecting the bright morning sunlight. Denim found herself impressed despite herself.

But as her focus suddenly landed on the figure of the man she knew was Brock Donovan, standing framed between the two enormous entranceway columns at the top of the wide steps, his knuckles bent firmly against his hips in stern acknowledgment of her approach, Denim experienced a sickening jolt of reality as she recalled how he had come to acquire this impressive display of his wealth.

She forced herself to speak cordially. "Mornin'."

Donovan's fierce gray eyebrows arched in a vain attempt at recognition.

Denim squinted under her Stetson. "Are you Mr. Donovan? Mr. Brock Donovan?"

Donovan nodded. "That I am. And who might you be?"

Denim brought Daybreaker to a halt but did not dismount. "Name's Laurie, sir," she said.

"Care for some coffee—Laurie?" Donovan offered.

"No, sir," Denim declined pleasantly. "Just come to talk to you."

Donovan's curiosity was aroused. "Well, lemme get one of the boys to park your horse and you can join me on the veranda."

"My horse is fine here, sir," Denim said, finally climbing down and giving Daybreaker's mane a quick brush. "He'll wait. 'Sides, I reckon what I got to say won't take long."

Donovan shrugged indifferently. "Suit yerself."

Denim whispered into Daybreaker's ear, stroked his neck, and gave his flank a sturdy pat, then started up the steps to the veranda. Donovan had already reseated himself at the breakfast table.

"There's nothin' better for the appetite than eatin' outdoors," he said expansively, if for no reason. He grabbed a piece of toast and spread a generous amount of marmalade over it.

Denim gave a quick, tight smile.

"Sit yourself," Donovan said to the girl, his tone suddenly brusque, suggesting an order rather than a polite invitation. He waved his hand to indicate the comfortable fan-backed chair across from him.

"If you don't mind, I'd rather stand," Denim returned.

Donovan shrugged, casually licking the marmalade from his fingers.

As she stared at the man who had betrayed her parents while he leisurely enjoyed his breakfast in the shade of his big house, Denim could feel every muscle in her body growing tense. Her soft blue eyes that could express such youthful innocence suddenly turned cold, their skylike hue turning cobalt. Her expression was rigid.

Brock Donovan took a moment to eye this girl stranger closely. He noticed the sudden tautness in her features.

She chose that moment to respond to his uncertainty. "Mr. Donovan, I rode out here to tell you that I aim to kill you." Strangely, her voice held no trace of menace; she spoke calmly, very matter-of-factly.

Donovan's face did not change expression other than a slight lifting of his thick, bushy eyebrows.

"Just so you know," Denim continued, firm in her stance, "I'm roomin' at the Prosperity Hotel. Room 201. I'm hopin' that you'll oblige me with a visit."

Donovan decided to let the girl play her game. His face widened with amusement. "Damn, I like yer spunk, girl. Spit an' vinegar. I'm sure you know I maintain strict rules 'bout ladyfolk walkin' around town unescorted. So I can see you're serious 'bout this . . . but it ain't to no one's benefit to make a claim agin my life. Have to ask you, though: why'd you'd chance comin' into my territory to, as you say, kill me?"

Denim's voice was as flat as her dead-eyed stare. "When the time's right, when you're starin' down the barrel of my gun, then you'll be admittin' to me what I know you done."

Brock Donovan was not a patient man and his tolerance was quickly reaching its limit. "Don't be talkin' riddles with me, girl. I could have you run outta town"—he snapped his fingers for emphasis—"as quick as that. Which I oughta do in any case for goin' agin my rule."

"I know all about them rules, Mr. Donovan. And that's just what you'll have to do, run me outta town," Denim said calmly. "But I'd be comin' back."

Donovan settled back in his seat. Despite his relaxed appearance Denim knew she had him worried—or at least got him to thinking. Donovan did indeed feel a strange chill rush up his spine as he realized that this wasn't a joke. That whoever this girl was . . . she did intend to kill him. He looked her over, decked out as she was in her blue jean outfit and cross-holster, and he quietly determined that she just might be capable of making good on her threat.

Still, he was confident with his own power, and his enormous pride would not let him succumb to fear from this prairie-dusted tart.

His lips pressed into a tight smile. "I don't aim to be

provokin' any fight with you, girl," he said. "And you best be rememberin' that if you should somehow make good on your threat, you'd be killin' me in cold blood. We have swift justice in Prosperity. Be a shame to see that pretty little body of yours strung up outside the courthouse."

"That don't frighten me a bit, Mr. Donovan," was all Denim said.

Donovan emitted a heavy breath and layered a spoonful of marmalade over another piece of toast. Denim noticed a slight trembling in his hands.

"I think you'd better be off my property," Donovan said, mildly yet firmly.

Denim hitched up her jeans, giving particular attention to the tugging of her gunbelt—for Donovan's benefit. "Aim to be doin' just that. I'm just givin' you fair warnin', Mr. Donovan. We'll be seein' each other agin—your way or mine. Within the week. That's my promise to you."

Denim turned and started to walk away. Donovan called after her, determined to have the last word in the matter.

"And lemme make a promise to *you*," he thundered. "I don't ride into town often. But if'n I should and I spot you still around, I'm gonna make it my business to see that you enjoy our jail facilities for a long time."

"On what charge?" Denim challenged, her back still facing him.

"Why, you just made a threat agin my life," Donovan replied unctuously. "I make the laws in Prosperity, little girl, and whether or not you know it, you just broke one.

Still, I'm in a generous mood this mornin'. So now I'm givin' *you* fair warnin'."

Donovan watched as the girl straddled her long legs over her mount before galloping off down the pathway. When she was gone from his sight, he sat back in his chair and remained there for a long time. Suddenly he broke out in a cold sweat. It wasn't that he was overly worried about the girl and her threat. He had protection for that. His concern was that the crimes of his past had apparently once more come back to haunt him. Crimes he neither wanted to be reminded of—nor have exposed.

The truth was that Brock Donovan was a tormented man. As he immersed himself deeper into the guise of respectability, he grew ever more fearful of his past betrayals being discovered. In recent months that fear of exposure transformed from worry into full-blown paranoia—and Donovan had decided upon measures that would eliminate all threats to the reputation he had strived so hard to establish.

Now Donovan found himself again forced into an extreme situation. The girl, whoever she was, surely knew of his past. As he saw it, there was no other reason why she would want to see him dead. Because of this, she would have to be dealt with promptly—and permanently.

Brock Donovan was an exceptionally careful man—even in the assigning of duties to his hired hands. While most of his men worked solely at their given tasks, Donovan also maintained a watchful eye and had chosen a select committee of men, such as Ned Randolph, to perform extra duties, for which they were paid generous cash bonuses. Certain property disputes, for instance, had to be handled personally, bypassing the jurisdiction of the sheriff's office, and Donovan called upon those trusted few to settle the problem—in whichever way the situation demanded. But these were usually simple affairs that his men could handle with a minimum of difficulty. Threats, occasionally a little persuasive force were all that was generally required to settle the argument—and always in Donovan's favor.

Donovan was cunning and ruthless, but he'd never bloodied his own hands by killing a man. In that he believed his conscience was clear. Yet he was aware of the need for someone who could carry out those "specialty" jobs. It required a talent not found among even the most able man in his employ. A specialty demanded a unique breed of individual. One who would charge a high price for his service, in return guaranteeing that the job would be handled cleanly and efficiently. While there was no shortage of eager young guns in the Southwest, Donovan knew there was only one man capable of handling these particular tasks.

He called in one of his men from the range and instructed him to ride into town and wire Tucson. He knew that was where Ben Straker would be making a stopover after completing his last assignment for him.

Chapter Seven

The Meeting

Denim could have shot Brock Donovan dead on the spot. She could have now been on the trail back to Caillou and her grandpa, satisfied that the debt she owed her parents had been paid in full. Instead she told Donovan of her intention and had given him a week to prepare. She did this partly to make him sweat with the realization that there was a personal bounty on his head. But Denim also knew that she could not kill the man outright until she heard him admit his guilt. She knew the truth would come. There was no mistaking the lifetime of evil she had seen reflected in Brock Donovan's eyes.

However, by allowing Donovan this period of reprieve, Denim knew that she had placed herself in a precarious situation. Donovan could now easily make the first move. Still, she intended to abide by the rules of fair play. She would kill him sure enough, but not murder him cold the way he deserved.

She had precious little time to fulfill what she had come to see as her destiny. During this period she would have to keep herself alert to every look and every action from those around her. She rode back into Prosperity with the understanding that to its citizens a favor received was a favor returned.

And she had seen for herself that Brock Donovan had the means to reward a lot of favors.

The next two days passed uneventfully for Denim. Her presence in town still evoked suspicious if not downright hostile stares, but no one troubled her. And no one spoke to her, except to pass whispered comments or to ridicule her 'boylike' appearance. Denim took it all in stride.

She'd come to believe that Donovan's threat to toss her in jail was an empty one. In fact, she was hoping that he'd underestimated her. By doing so, he was giving her the time she needed to prepare for that moment when he would walk into her bullet.

Besides Marie DuBois, there was one other person in Prosperity with whom Denim had formed a friendly acquaintance. That was Tom Becker who ran the livery stable. At first as resistant to her as everyone else in town, Tom's shared love of horses and an admiration for the beauty and intelligence of Daybreaker soon opened conversation between himself and Denim when she would come in each morning to groom her horse.

On this particular sun-drenched August morning Tom ambled in while Denim was inside the stall cleaning out Daybreaker's nostrils with a damp sponge. The horse occasionally snorted but was agreeable to the procedure.

Tom watched the girl briefly, then released a chuckle.

Denim turned around. "Mornin'," she greeted.

"Take your horse out yet?" Tom inquired.

"Just brought him back from a run." Denim examined the sponge, popped a breath, and then shook her head. "Can you believe I'm still cleanin' out grit from the Tellahu?" she remarked.

Tom chuckled again. "Yeh, and probably will for a while," he told her. "After what you told me, still surprises the bejesus out of me that the two of you ever made it out of the desert."

"Mr. Tom Becker, there ain't nothin' the two of us can't get ourselves through," Denim said with a burst of exaggerated pride.

Tom began sauntering through the stable inspecting the feeding racks. "How long you plannin' to stay in Prosperity?" he asked casually.

Denim suspected the reason for his question.

"Reckon people have a lot to say," she said quietly, soaking a fresh sponge inside the water pail and starting to carefully wipe around Daybreaker's eyes.

Tom pulled a strip of jerky from his shirt pocket and bit off a piece. He moved toward the outside of the stall. "Y'gotta understand. Not much happens in Prosperity. You're a topic for conversation."

Denim answered his original question curtly. "Just got some business to take care of, then I'll be on my way."

"What them others may be sayin' ain't necessarily the way I feel," Tom was quick to add. "Live and let be, that's my motto."

Denim heaved a sigh. "I know that, Mr. Becker," she said appreciatively.

"It's just what everyone around here seems to want to know," Tom explained, chewing hard on his jerky, which was quite a task considering that he was missing most of his teeth.

"Reckon they figure havin' a woman around is bad luck?" Denim surmised with a wry smile. " 'Less, of course, she's a saloon girl."

"Strange town, strange folks," Tom replied. "What it is, why you're here . . . that's your own affair."

Denim squeezed the moisture from the sponge onto the ground and laid it atop a post. With her back facing Tom, she slowly and smoothly brushed her hands dry against the curve of her buttocks, down the faded tight fit of her jeans. She did not turn to notice the glint that appeared in old Tom's eyes or the subtle smile that crept across his lips.

Instead she said in a straightforward manner: "Tom Becker, I can only tell you this: When I do ride outta Prosperity, everyone's gonna know I'd been here."

Tom Becker's ancient face became animated as it registered a variety of expressions, finally settling on a look of bewildered acceptance.

The sound of a limping hoofbeat was heard against the wood-planked floor of the stable.

Both Denim and Tom turned at the approach. They noticed a silhouette against the glare of the late-morning sun slowly leading a mount inside the structure. The horse clopped forward with a sharp arching of its right foreleg.

"You in charge here?" the stranger asked Tom Becker.

"I is," Tom replied, squinting. "What's wrong with your horse?"

"Don't know," the stranger said as he stepped deeper into the stable, making himself fully visible to both Denim and Tom. "His leg started acting up this morning. I thought it might be a sprain of some sort so I walked him in from outside of town."

"It ain't no sprain," Denim said conclusively as she walked round from inside the stall. "Looks to me like he's got somethin' stuck in his hoof."

She only glanced at the stranger before giving her full attention to the horse.

For the stranger, however, his first good look at the girl struck him like a thunderbolt.

There was no way he could not know who she was. He'd carried her image with him the first time he had ever laid eyes on her—riding on the Sam Abbott Wild West circuit. The girl called *Denim Ryder*.

"You think you can help her?" he politely asked the girl.

Denim did not answer. She went over to the animal and lowered to a crouch, speaking gentle words before she examined its favored hoof.

Daybreaker suddenly neighed and stomped his foot.

"Quiet there, Daybreaker," Denim scolded over her shoulder.

"Think your horse might be a bit jealous," Tom Becker observed with a chuckle.

"He is," Denim returned.

"Hee-hee, that's some horse," Tom said.

"Mistuh," Denim finally said to the stranger. "I ain't never seen hooves this neglected. This one here's so overgrown its jammed tight with mesquite thorns and all. When's the last time you had these shoes replaced?"

"I—don't rightfully know," the stranger admitted, somewhat timidly.

For the first time Denim looked straight up at the stranger. She was ready to lambaste him good for not properly caring for his horse, but when her eyes fell completely upon his smooth, handsome features she was momentarily taken aback, much to her own discomfort. She made herself swiftly recover.

"You don't know!" she chided. "How'd you think you'd feel walkin' 'round with a bootful of cactus?"

The stranger was slow in replying. "Just . . . never gave it much thought, ma'am."

Denim had turned her concern back to the horse. "I ain't no ma'am," she muttered under her breath. Then she spoke with a little more emphasis. "Name's Laurie."

The stranger managed a tentative smile. "Reckon I'm not much of a cowboy—*Laurie*," he said.

Denim pivoted her head just enough to take another

look at this fellow, paying particular notice of the clothes he was wearing. He certainly wasn't a cowboy; he looked every inch the city dude.

"No argument here," she was quick to agree.

The stranger stood there, quietly acknowledging the strangeness of the situation. Denim Ryder had no way of knowing how grateful he was for his little misfortune with his horse.

Denim rose from her crouch and placed her fists firmly against her hips. She shook her head. "These shoes gotta be replaced." She turned to Tom Becker. "Anyone in town who can handle that?"

Tom laughed mischievously. "And little lady, whaddaya think I do?'

"You're a farrier!" Denim exclaimed. She flipped off her Stetson and gave it a sharp slap against her thigh. "So why didn't you just say so?" she said with mock irritation.

"Thought you was doin' a purty good job yourself," Tom replied, amused.

The stranger sighed. "Well, I suppose that's going to take a while."

Tom Becker flicked his eyes from the stranger to Denim. "A while," he said. Then with a crafty smile: "Maybe longer."

The stranger understood. He acknowledged Tom's subtle suggestion by casting a pleasant glance toward Denim, who was shyly trying to avert her eyes from his attention. "Any chance you'll have it done by, say, dinner?" he asked.

"Dinner?" Tom scrunched his forehead. "I was thinkin' 'bout the breakfast they got down at the hotel."

Denim was clearly perplexed. She busily scratched her scalp. "Dinner? Breakfast? What're you two talkin' 'bout?'

"If I may," the stranger explained, "our friend here is suggesting that I might occupy my wait by sharing your company."

"Huh?" Denim said, still not fully understanding. *This fella sure talks fancy,* she thought.

"Durn it, girl," Tom cut in impatiently. "He wants to buy you a meal."

"It's the least I can do after the care you're giving Dixie," the stranger said with a warm smile.

"But—Mr. Becker's doin' all the work," Denim protested.

"Yes. And as much as I appreciate Mr. Becker's efforts, I believe I would enjoy your company more."

"But I already et," Denim said, lifting a shoulder.

"So much the better," the stranger said, undaunted. "I do have an errand to run, and, besides, I'd much prefer to treat you to a full-course dinner at the hotel—if Mr. Becker thinks Dixie might need to rest her foot a while afterward."

"Oh, I'd keep her rested a spell, surely would," Tom concurred in a swift voice.

"In the meantime, I'll be needing a horse," the stranger said to Tom.

"I can fix you up with one," Tom offered. "Cost you a dollar."

"So—you're askin' me to have supper with you?" Denim

said, still unsure and now a little wary of the stranger's intention.

"Yes. If you'll favor me with your charming company."

"But I—I don't even know you," Denim stammered. "Don't even know your name."

"And a proper introduction certainly is in order, Laurie." The stranger dipped in a slight bow. "The name is Benjamin."

Denim was at a loss. This invitation had come upon her too suddenly and she did not know how to properly respond. She did find this fella Benjamin a good-looking sort, and he sure had fine and fancy manners. And she was flattered by his attention and offer of dinner. But she had to remind herself that she had a specific purpose for riding into Prosperity—one that she could not compromise by falling for the overtures of an attractive man.

She started to decline. "I thank you for your invitation. I 'preciate it, but . . ."

"I assure you, I'm not a man to pressure, Laurie," Benjamin quickly interjected.

Denim felt herself getting all turned around. She struggled to at least offer him an explanation. "It's a might kind gesture. Only . . . only it don't fit in with what I'm here for."

"No need for a reason," Benjamin assured her. "But I've got to ride back for dinner anyway. Should be back around six. I'll be seated at the restaurant in the Prosperity Hotel. In the event you might change your mind, I'll set aside a table for two. But that'll be completely your decision. I will say, though, that I hope you change your mind."

Denim smiled sweetly and lowered her gaze to the stable floor. Her cheeks blushed and her dimples showed. As if against her will she felt herself beginning to surrender to her feminine side, that part of her she admittedly rarely acknowledged, and the one most vulnerable to Benjamin's undeniable charm.

"I—can't promise exactly," she began to say.

"Fair enough," Benjamin responded, his own dimples showing as he grinned.

Denim felt the matter was settled. "Well, okay. So long as that's an understandin', and there ain't no hard feelins if'n I don't come."

Tom Becker was snickering and having a grand time witnessing this exchange. He'd never started his day expecting to be a matchmaker. In fact, he really did not know why he had even interfered. Except, he reckoned, that the girl could use another friend in an unfriendly town.

Benjamin looked at his jovial expression and spoke with mock irritation. "Look, old man, if you don't want to get saddled with the dinner bill, I'd suggest you shuffle on outta here and fix me up with that horse."

"Oh, yessir, yessir." Tom giggled as he went deliberately around the couple and walked outside into the corral to pick a suitable mount.

"What d'you say you call your horse?" Denim asked Benjamin.

"Not my horse," Benjamin returned with a smile. "But her name is Dixie."

"Dixie," she murmured. "That's a right purty name."

"I like it," Benjamin agreed. "And maybe if we do get together tonight, you could give me some tips on how to better care for her."

Denim gave a faint, shy smile but didn't reply.

She and Benjamin found themselves alone for a moment, each gazing silently at the other, though Denim's eyes occasionally drifted. She was uncertain, tentative, and she soon completely turned her face away, though in doing so she stood poised in the spill of the morning sunlight that filtered into the stable through the cracked opening of an outer wall. The broken golden ray splashed a glow across her features, against which she stood with slightly closed eyes, this giving her face a soft, almost ethereal look. Benjamin stood transfixed by her beauty, aware that the simple perfection of this moment would forever stay in his memory.

What went without saying, what the young man firmly resolved never to risk revealing, was his identity. That he, who called himself Benjamin, was the notorious killer-for-hire Ben Straker. Benjamin was the name he adopted to win his victims' trust—the name he had been called growing up as a child of privilege and propriety. Out of necessity he had evolved Benjamin into a completely separate personality. He had traveled long distances and had met his share of people, a few of whom "Benjamin" could have taken a liking to if Ben Straker wasn't professionally bound to kill them. Those who on occasion he had been required to briefly befriend before betraying them with a bullet. Perhaps Benjamin could have remembered the faces of these men—but not Ben Straker. They were erased from his memory once the job was done. This was how he had to operate . . . how he survived at his work. His creed was simple: no commitments. No attachments.

But from the first time he'd seen the girl named Denim Ryder trick riding her mount and sharpshooting glass balls in an open arena in Texas, she had taken a special, permanent spot in his thoughts. Ben Straker could never have dreamed that he would be standing next to the girl he had admired so long from afar. He actually felt his heart flutter with the giddiness of a lovestruck teenager. A reaction totally at odds with the type of person Ben Straker was. But to a man for whom emotions could not be permitted, this was a feeling not easily ignored.

Neither spoke for those moments that they were alone. When Tom Becker came back inside to tell Benjamin that he had found him a good horse, Benjamin did not even say good-bye to the girl. Because to him it was not good-bye. Only a temporary parting. He simply smiled and gave his head a polite nod. Denim returned the smile, unaware that her eyes were now sparkling.

Denim stepped over to the stable door and carefully kept herself hidden from sight as she watched Benjamin saddle the chestnut-colored Morgan. He mounted the unfamiliar animal, carefully easing his feet into the stirrups, and then tested the horse with a slow trot through the corral before riding off to wherever his destination. Denim stood there for a while before returning to Daybreaker's stall to finish grooming him. Her mind was a muddle of thoughts, and after some consideration she decided to go have a talk with her friend Marie DuBois.

After first checking the saloon, where Joe McDonald at least had the courtesy to answer "No" when she asked him if he'd seen Marie, Denim next went over to the hotel, where she found Marie sipping a cup of tea off in the corner of the cozy dining room.

The Prosperity Hotel dining room was where on Saturdays, the one day when "respectable" women were permitted to ride in unescorted from the valley to shop or just enjoy a leisurely afternoon in town, men and their wives, bedecked in fancy wear, would eat from a special menu in candelit elegance. The dining room would close at 9:30, after which the men might send their well-fed wives home while they partook of less sedate "entertainment" at the Golden Circle Saloon. Throughout the week, the restaurant served as more of a coffee shop, frequented by merchants, farmers, and cowboys, usually come to discuss business or just to shoot the breeze.

It was Tuesday just before noon, and Marie was the only customer in the place, though some of the regulars would soon be coming in for lunch. She could tell immediately that Denim was eager to speak with her. The girl rushed over to her table and spun the chair across from her back-forward, seating herself before waiting to be invited. Denim quickly, almost breathlessly, began telling her about the handsome stranger Benjamin. Marie listened patiently.

Marie did not speak until Denim had said everything she had wanted to say. Then she simply asked: "Benjamin. That his first name or his last?"

Denim looked perplexed, and a bit embarrassed. "I—never asked," she said meekly. "Just called himself Benjamin."

"Sounds to me like you met someone you may have taken a fancy to," Marie remarked, sounding pleased.

However, despite the enthusiasm in her telling, Denim suddenly did not want to acknowledge that possibility. "No," she said, almost abruptly. Then she softened. "It ain't that at all," she said as she twisted restlessly in her chair. "Heck, I ain't sure what it is, but I do know it ain't nothin' I should be considerin' right now. It's kinda hard to explain, ma'am." She took a moment to gather her thoughts, then leaned forward across the table. "Y'see, remember when I told you that I came to this town for a purpose? Well, I still can't tell you what I come for, but it's somethin' I gotta keep my head clear for—without no complications."

"Sounds serious," Marie said as she poured the last drops of tea from the china pot into her cup.

"It is," Denim said with conviction. "And because I just gotta see it through, I can't have no interferences."

"And you feel this Benjamin might get in your way?" Marie conjectured.

Denim narrowed her eyes as she contemplated her answer.

"Don't know," she said quietly. "But it ain't somethin' I can afford to chance."

Marie spoke frankly. "Denim, you're a beautiful girl. You're talented and you seem to have good sense. You've obviously accomplished a lot in your young life. But from the first time I met you I saw someone not quite sure of who she is. Of who she wants to be. You rode through the desert to the most male-dominated town in the Southwest, put yourself up to ridicule by your attitude and the way you dress, all because you say you've got some purpose. Whatever that purpose is, it's got a grip on you that's preventing *Laurie* Ryder from being happy. The sad fact is, sometimes you're only given that one chance to find happiness."

Denim was both puzzled and impressed by her friend's perception. "How'd you figure all that out?" she asked with a frown.

Marie wore a melancholy smile. "You're not the first girl I've talked to like this."

Denim lowered her eyes. "But I can't be turnin' back from what I gotta do," she stated firmly.

Marie sighed. "Then it sounds to me like you've made up your mind regarding that fella."

Denim paused. Then she looked up at Marie and frowned again. "Ain't sure that I have."

Marie reached her arm across the table and cupped her hand over the girl's wrist, which was dangling over the back of the chair. "Denim, only *you* know what's right for you. But one thing you should keep in mind: Accepting a gentleman's invitation to dinner doesn't have to mean more than that."

Denim nodded. "I reckon you're right. Just havin' a meal can't hurt."

"But honey," Marie said gently and with a smile, "you can't be sharing the company of a gentleman unless you present yourself in more suitable dress."

Denim briefly pondered her advice, finally replying: "If I'm only goin' to be eatin' with him, don't see what difference my clothes make."

Marie just shook her head and said in mock exasperation: "Denim, you and I are going to have a long talk."

Later that afternoon as a mud-gray cloud bank rolled heavy over the eastern mountain ridge, perhaps an indication of much-needed rain, Ben Straker rode up to Brock Donovan's sprawling ranch house.

Donovan's greeting to Ben was, as usual, guarded. Donovan was a man who took pleasure in flaunting his authority over the families that resided in the valley, and for most of these folks such subservience was a small price for the comfortable living his "generosity" had afforded them. Yet Ben Straker was one man who even Brock Donovan treated with respect. This was due, of course, to the gunman's reputation. In their professional dealings, Donovan would first determine Straker's frame of mind before deciding on the best way to approach the business at hand. If Straker welcomed cordiality, Donovan would offer it. If Straker was not in a talkative mood, Donovan would likewise dismiss with pleasantries. Today Ben Straker seemed in an uncharacteristically receptive mood, so Donovan took advantage of his good nature to put himself firmly in control.

Donovan perhaps had another reason to feel confident. As Ben entered the spaciousness of the parlor, he noted that Sheriff Tom Brough was also present, seated comfortably in an overstuffed armchair at the back of the room. Ben couldn't see the reason for Brough being there; to his recollection, the sheriff had no official authority beyond that which Donovan dictated. But Brough certainly presented an intimidating figure—a man as large, if not larger, than Donovan, but muscular rather than fat. Ben could freely admit that in any physical confrontation Brough could snap him in half like a matchstick. Brough regarded Ben with a slight tilt of his head before returning to his drink. It was clear he would be excluded from this conversation.

"You did a good job for me at Caillou," Donovan said as he went to pour Ben a drink.

Ben had never before been invited to Donovan's house. When they discussed 'business' they usually met at secluded spots chosen by Donovan, generally outside the territory. In fact, Ben had never even ventured into Donovan's town before. Which was the way he preferred it. A town where he knew no one . . . and no one knew who he was.

Ben's eyes traveled the expanse of the parlor, which possessed a cold, impersonal atmosphere—much like the man himself—finally settling on the animal head trophies that were mounted on the wall over the fireplace. Wild beasts: eyes flashing their silent rage, mouths agape, fangs prominently displayed. Ben wondered whether Donovan attached a value to these grotesqueries beyond mere ornamentation. If maybe in Donovan's mind they stood as symbols of his conquests in the building of his empire, representing those who had defied him, and who he had crushed to establish and maintain his position. It wasn't much different from the ritual observed by many who shared Ben's trade: the carving of notches on revolver handles or rifle stocks to keep score of kills.

"Must have been an important man," Ben mused sardonically, remembering the old, simple farmer he had shot in the back of the head.

Donovan noted but ignored his sarcasm. He merely looked over at Tom Brough.

He walked across to Ben and handed him a snifter of brandy. He himself was holding a full glass of bourbon.

"Just a loose end," he said dismissively.

Ben took a gentlemanly sip of his drink. It was fine brandy. Another standard of Brock Donovan's prominence.

"Now you want me to kill a girl," he said musingly. He knew the girl was the old man's granddaughter and the fact intrigued him. But he did not question Donovan on it. He made it a rule never to question his employers' motives.

Donovan's eyes flashed. "She's given me no choice!" he exclaimed defensively.

Ben nodded. "I've already seen her," he offered. "In fact, I'm hoping to have dinner with her this evening. Name's Laurie."

Donovan placed no importance on the name. He merely walked over to the big stone fireplace and gazed into the hearth.

"And she's not one you want to be tangling with," Ben advised. He settled back into his chair and crossed his legs, assuming a relaxed pose. "I've seen her handle a gun."

Donovan coughed, a little obviously, but he maintained his pose of authority.

"I didn't build all this," he said with a wide, sweeping gesture of his meaty hands to indicate his house and property holdings, "by being a-scared of little girls."

Ben was not impressed. Donovan never impressed him in any way, shape or form. And despite Donovan's protestation, Ben knew that he *was* afraid.

He regarded his brandy. "Still . . . I've never been asked to handle something like this."

Donovan regarded him tauntingly. "What're you sayin? You can't do it . . . or you *won't*?"

Ben would not allow his professionalism to be questioned. Maintaining control, he slowly raised half-closed eyelids toward Donovan, fixing him with a cold stare.

"You've never had reason to be dissatisfied with my work, Mr. Donovan," he said. "And if you have doubts now—why, you've got the law here to take care of it." There was just the tiniest note of contempt in Ben's voice as he flicked his eyes toward Tom Brough, who sat impassively, his expression flat.

Donovan chilled at Ben's expression, about as inviting as an open coffin. But his apprehension was such that he made himself speak with forced aggression. "This goes beyond the law," he growled. "This little spitfire rides into town threatenin' to put a bullet into me."

He waited for Ben Straker's response, which did not come. But Ben sat back in his chair with a growing interest. He saw the pieces of the puzzle come together—even if Donovan remained frustrated by the riddle.

Steadying himself, Donovan sought to ease the palpable tension developing between them by bringing the decanter of brandy over to Ben to freshen his drink. Ben cupped a hand over the glass and gave his head a slow shake. He took to describing Denim, reciting each detail with deliberate emphasis to gauge Donovan's reaction. "Young girl, maybe early twenties, but looks younger. Blond. Pretty as all tomorrow. Seems to have a likin' for jean wear."

"That's her," Donovan snarled. His hand flexed, crushing the glass that he held. He winced as he noticed thin rivulets of blood tracking across his palm. He pulled out the handkerchief from the breast pocket of his coat and wrapped it around the wound.

"Sounds like you're keen on the girl," he said, fixing his attention on his makeshift bandage, checking for leakage.

"You might say that," Ben said effortlessly.

Donovan spoke craftily. "Talk like that makes me question your loyalty."

Ben was becoming bored with the conversation. "Pay my price, Mr. Donovan, and you don't need to have any concerns," he said simply.

Donovan allowed himself to relax a little. He again checked the bleeding through his kerchief, then went to pour himself a fresh drink.

He moved back to the fireplace. "Maybe your gettin' together with her ain't necessarily a bad thing," he said contemplatively.

Ben sat quietly, waiting to hear him out.

Donovan considered the situation. "She came here for a purpose—" he began to say.

"To see you dead," Ben interjected, deadpan.

Donovan hardly appreciated Ben's bluntness. He scowled at him. "Yeh." He pondered for a moment. "But I gotta know why. What she's got agin me." He pointed a finger directly at Ben. "Spend some time with her and find out."

Ben rocked his head. Then he played his advantage. "I might be able to get what you want. But I think in this case it'll cost you a premium."

Donovan walked away from the fireplace. He gulped a swallow from his glass of bourbon and said impatiently: "I'm not concerned 'bout the money, Straker. I want this done right. Get me what I want and I'll . . . double your pay."

Now Ben was impressed with Donovan. "That's a might generous offer."

Donovan's charcoal eyes grew hard. "Just don't grow

too sweet on her, Ben. Once you find out what you can, I expect you to finish the job."

Ben Straker's face remained a study in control: cool, impassive, giving no hint to what was going on in his brain. Unlike Donovan, when it came to 'business' matters he allowed *nothing* to show. No display of doubt, concern, or vulnerability. Donovan noticed how his face never changed expression—not even when he was told his assignment was a girl.

Ben was indeed conscious of this. But there was no disguising what was going through his brain. And the grim irony that the girl he was being asked to kill was Denim Ryder, the only girl he felt he could ever have a true caring for.

The only girl he believed he could ever love.

After Ben Straker left the ranch to ride back into town, followed soon after by Tom Brough, Brock Donovan settled into his overstuffed easy chair and sipped on the rest of his drink. His apprehensions eased thanks to the relaxing effects of the bourbon and his deal with Ben. The girl would no longer be a concern to him . . .

But the anguished shriek that suddenly carried through the cavernous rooms of the house, shattering the calm and disturbing his reverie, was a horrible reminder of the one concern he could not so easily remove from his life.

Brock Donovan was a man of many dark secrets. The one secret that he most jealously guarded was locked away inside a back corner room of the house.

Acknowledging the cry, Donovan braced himself by finishing off his drink, then he rose from the comfort of his chair and walked slowly down the hall to where the scream had emanated. His house servant, a man named Chester, the only person to whom Donovan entrusted his secret, was already standing outside the door to the locked room. He held the key in his hand.

"I'll tend to her," Donovan said to the elderly man as he took the key from him. His voice was both tentative and gentle.

Another piercing shriek rose from inside the room.

"Maybe you should let me go inside, Mr. Donovan," Chester said cautiously. "You know what can happen when she gets like this."

Donovan did know. The woman behind that door was beyond reason: inconsolable in her periods of intense sorrow; violent and unmanageable in her sudden outbursts of rage. Only Chester seemed to have the ability to soothe her. He would sing gently to her, holding her in his arms and rocking her, and soon her face would relax its horrific contortions and perhaps just a spark of sanity, of recognition and an acknowledgment to his kindness, would momentarily return to eyes that had long ago lost their comprehension.

Donovan hesitated. And then he handed Chester back the key. He knew his servant was right. As difficult as it was for him to admit, Donovan had to acknowledge that the union they had once shared no longer existed. The person she had once been—the vibrant young girl who had devoted her life and her love to him—was no more. What Donovan was now forced to keep locked behind that heavy wood door only served as another reminder of a past he wanted forgotten. But what Donovan found most difficult to accept was that the shell of a woman he kept forever imprisoned inside that far corner bedroom—his *wife*, Elizabeth—had become the most tragic victim of his many cruelties, and a most personal betrayal from which she had been forever scarred.

Chapter Eight

The Courting

Benjamin had washed and changed his clothes and was seated at a reserved table for two in the dining room of the Prosperity Hotel. He nursed a glass of brandy and spooned a bowl of chicken giblet soup while he waited with anticipation and not a little apprehension to see whether his guest would arrive. He snapped open the gold casing of the pocket watch he had taken into his possession and glanced at the time. It was 6:35. He wore an unconscious frown. Then his expression mellowed as he again took a moment to admire the photograph of the smiling Denim Ryder affixed to the inside cover before carefully concealing the watch inside his coat pocket.

The waiter came to the table to inquire whether Benjamin was ready to order dinner. Benjamin hesitated, and sighed. He said that he was. But before he could take another cursory look at the menu, he saw out the corner of his eye a slim, faded blue-clad figure walking into the restaurant.

Denim was immediately stopped at the be-draped entrance by the manager, Maurice. He was a fussy man of impeccable manners and an adopted Continental accent that was as phony as his name. His real name was Morris Blumholz, a chef from San Francisco whose pretended class had so impressed Brock Donovan that he had brought the man to Prosperity to upgrade both the ambience and cuisine of his hotel restaurant. While as much a fish out of water in Prosperity as was Denim, Maurice still spoke to her in a condescending tone.

"During the day we hold no code on proper dress. And since you are, ahem, a friend of Madam DuBois, we do permit other, uh . . . exceptions, as well. But for dinner we *must* insist on more formal attire."

Denim, who towered over the meticulous little man, grinned and nodded agreeably, finding his pretentious manner quite funny.

Benjamin, however, was not so amused. He tolerated Maurice's insulting manner for only a few moments before he got up from the table, ignoring the protests of his waiter, who could only sigh in exasperation, and walked toward them.

He fixed the slight restaurant manager with an icy stare. "The lady is dining with me," he said bluntly.

Maurice's face went pale. He recognized this 'gentleman' from his periodic visits to the gambling house he had serviced in San Francisco. More importantly, he knew of his reputation. Maintaining house rules was one thing; risking insult to the most notorious gunman in the Southwest was quite another.

He recovered, resuming his professional demeanor.

"Certainly, Mr. Stra—" Maurice began to say in his most officious tone before Benjamin flashed him a look that instantly quieted him.

"That's fine," Benjamin said, still regarding the man with a cold expression. "I'll escort the lady to our table."

Benjamin took Denim by the arm and walked her to their quiet arrangement in a far corner of the room and pulled out a chair for her. The girl looked at him with a curious expression. She wasn't being rude; she simply was not familiar with such courtesy. Benjamin gestured for her to take the seat. Denim sat, sliding the chair forward herself before Benjamin could do it for her.

Benjamin took his own seat across from her. He spoke without sounding critical. "I suppose our friend did have a point. You didn't exactly dress for the occasion."

"My friend Marie tried to fix me up in somethin', but I don't take to no fancy dressin'," Denim replied in a straightforward manner. She then reached across the table for a slice of bread, which she lathered with butter, quickly consuming it.

"Hungry?" Benjamin asked, quietly amused.

Denim spoke with her mouth full. "Famished. Ain't really et since breakfast."

Benjamin caught the critical looks of a few other diners as they watched the girl devour the bread with all the grace of a buzzard consuming its prey.

Still, despite her lack of etiquette and inappropriate dress, Benjamin thought she looked beautiful and was pleased to share her company. "I'm glad you decided to come," he said.

Denim wiped around her mouth with her napkin. "Wasn't sure if I should."

"What made you decide?" Benjamin asked, curious.

Before Denim could come up with an answer, the waiter again came to the table. He looked irritated and drew a prolonged breath.

Benjamin's eyes never left the girl. "I guess we should order," he said to her.

Denim studied the menu, unable to understand most of its offerings. This, of course, further stretched the fraying patience of their server. Ben finally suggested that he place the order for both of them. Denim agreed.

"Even on the circuit I don't eat this fancy," she said as she set down the menu.

Benjamin decided on two fifty-cent dinners of roast loin of beef, along with a side order of "Arizona strawberries" (dried red beans). This sounded acceptable to Denim, who nodded her okay. Ben asked if she'd care for a drink. She replied: "A sarsaparilla." Again the waiter did not look pleased; the restaurant had a fine liquor menu. Benjamin said firmly to him: "A sarsaparilla for the lady."

"Very good, sir."

"Make that *two* sarsaparillas," Benjamin added.

The waiter turned from the table, rolled his eyes, and hurried into the kitchen.

"That fella looks to be in the wrong line of work," Denim remarked. "Kinda nervous."

Benjamin smiled at her. The dining room was dimly lit and he was admiring Denim through the flicker of light supplied by the candlepiece centered on their table. He was about to comment on how lovely she looked when Denim spoke first.

She threw an arm over the back of her chair and said: "I been meanin' to ask you. Benjamin . . . is that your first name or your last?"

"Is that important?" Benjamin replied.

"Well . . . I'm sittin' here eatin' with you," Denim said with a shrug. "Should know who it is I'm with."

"Benjamin is my surname. Walter Benjamin. Never cared for Walter so I took to using Benjamin."

"Can't say I care for either Walter or Benjamin," Denim said honestly. "Don't mind Ben, though."

"Ben would be fine," he said. He again asked: "What made you decide to join me tonight?"

Denim seemed stumped for an answer. "I—reckon I been askin' myself the same question," she finally replied.

"Yet here you are," Benjamin said, resisting the temptation to reach over and take her hand.

"I know," she said delicately.

Benjamin didn't pursue the topic. He felt he did not need to. He had not mistaken the way she'd looked at him earlier, when they were alone in the stable. There was no mistaking the unspoken attraction they felt for one another. She was here with him now simply because she wanted to be.

And while she was hesitant to voice it, Denim was indeed attracted to the man who called himself Benjamin. His handsome features, his good manners, and gentle behavior toward her. He treated her with the same kindness and respect she'd been told her father had treated her mother. The father she often wished she had known.

Perhaps at a different time Denim could have loosened the grip on her restraints to welcome the courtship of a man like Benjamin. But presently her independence and need for self-preservation were qualities strong within her. She had to remind herself that whatever she was feeling toward Benjamin could go no further than their sharing a dinner together.

As the evening progressed, Benjamin could see how Denim was holding herself back. When he'd ask her a question about herself she would politely answer in as few words as possible. She confessed her identity as Denim Ryder and talked a bit about her life on the rodeo circuit while Ben feigned ignorance regarding her accomplishments.

Denim seemed grateful when her meal arrived so that she could give it her full attention and thereby preclude conversation. She immediately dug into her food with purpose while Benjamin merely picked at his dinner. He refused to surrender to an uncomfortable silence. He finally decided to encourage talk by shifting the topic to what he knew held an interest for her: horses.

Benjamin broached the subject casually, but Denim, to his surprise and delight, opened up immediately. The love she felt for horses, and Daybreaker in particular, was clear, and while he could not share her knowledge, he managed to keep the conversation going. Finally, as they neared the end of their meal, he asked Denim outright if she might consider riding with him tomorrow. She stopped short and again seemed reluctant to give an answer.

"I'm asking if you would like to go riding tomorrow," Benjamin repeated.

"Your horse ain't up for no ridin'," Denim very quickly replied.

"No," Benjamin said. "But I rode a fine Morgan today. I'm sure I can persuade that old stable hand to let me take her out again tomorrow."

When Denim did not immediately respond, instead picking at her empty plate with her fork, Benjamin added: "I've got to be moving on in a couple of days. My work rarely keeps me in one place for long. Don't get much of a chance to enjoy such company as yours."

Denim refused to lift her eyes from the plate. "I'll be on my way soon too," she muttered. "It's just that . . . well, it ain't that simple."

Benjamin tried to reassure her. "If you're hesitating because you think I'm looking for something beyond a few days' companionship . . ."

Denim finally raised her blue eyes to Benjamin and

regarded him with an innocent look. Then reality again set in and she lowered her gaze. A man had to die. A price had to be paid. Denim could not forget the obligation she owed her parents. And especially now as she had finally seen and spoke with Brock Donovan, and she knew it would be a pleasure to kill him.

At the same time, she remembered what Marie had said to her. How she had been denying herself the right to be happy because she had become obsessed with what she had to do. These conflicting thoughts caused her head to start to spin—almost as if she had been drinking something stronger than sarsaparilla. She had never felt this way before. Both urges tugged at her, and while Denim Ryder could not deny one, Laurie Ryder found herself very much wanting to acknowledge the other.

Which, almost against her will, she did.

"I usually take Daybreaker out for a run around nine," she told Benjamin. "You're welcome to join me if'n you'd like."

"I look forward to it—Laurie," Benjamin said.

They rode together in pleasurable rhythm, side by side across the drifting grasslands, under clear azure skies just dabbed with cottony puffs of clouds. The mountains stood low on the horizon, a reminder to Denim that she was far from where she most wanted to be.

Then—she suddenly snapped Daybreaker into a swift run. She raced her mount up over the rolling hills that overlooked the valley. Denim rode with a competitive spirit, while Benjamin was content to hold back and admire her equestrian skills. Finally they met at the crest of one of the rises.

"I'm impressed," Benjamin said to her.

"Been on a horse all my life," Denim replied, invigorated by the ride. She gazed out into the openness of the Wabowda Valley, then took in a deep breath, clearing her head as well as her lungs. "You can almost taste the air," she said. "And it tastes sweet. You almost wouldn't expect to find such country here in the desert."

Benjamin played ignorant. "You're not from the valley?" he asked.

Denim shook her head, her long blond hair blowing in the gentle breeze. "Thought I told you. I come south of here. Place called Caillou."

Benjamin blinked, but was careful not to offer any other expression.

"What brings you here?" he asked, maintaining a casual interest.

"Personal business," Denim replied shortly.

"Prosperity is kind of a strange town for a girl to be riding into by herself," Benjamin remarked.

"So I've found out," Denim said absently. She hastened to change the subject. "Now, why don't you tell me 'bout yourself, Walter Benjamin?"

Benjamin grinned. "I'm a man of no secrets. What would you like to know?"

Denim thought quickly. "Where you're from, for instance. What you do."

"I'm from up East. Boston, to be precise, which I figure accounts for my lack of horse sense," Benjamin said, enjoying Denim's wide, dimple-enhancing grin in response to his joke. "As to how I make my living . . . I guess you could call me sort of a troubleshooter."

"Troubleshooter?" Denim asked with a puzzled look.

"I, uh, take care of other people's problems," Benjamin explained.

"Kinda sounds like a gunslinger," Denim said kiddingly.

Benjamin kept his face from reddening. "Kinda," he replied with an innocuous smile.

Both fell into silence. Finally Benjamin fidgeted and spoke what was foremost on his mind. "Laurie, I'd appreciate your telling me if I'm speaking out of line, but—contrary to what I said before . . . I find myself becoming mighty attracted to you. Reckon what I'm saying is . . . I'd like to get to know you better."

Denim remained quiet for a moment longer. "Mr. Benjamin," she then said, "it ain't that I don't find your attention flatterin', but now just ain't the time for me to be thinkin' 'bout no involvement."

Ben Straker understood what she was saying. It was as much a reminder to himself. Whatever his personal feelings toward the girl, he too had a commitment. The girl that he wanted at that moment to sweep into his arms and embrace with all the passion he possessed was first and foremost a professional assignment. By week's end she had made a promise to kill Brock Donovan. Before that could happen, he was expected to kill her.

Still, his desire was deep, his words not a mere affectation.

"I'm a patient man, Miss Ryder" was all he said.

Denim smiled demurely and snapped Daybreaker into a gallop. Benjamin spurred his mount to follow, this time not holding back. He swiftly followed down the hill and through the tall grasses that blanketed the curving slope. When he finally pulled his horse alongside Denim, the girl drew her thighs tight against Daybreaker's flanks, bringing the animal to a halt. Benjamin noticed this play of muscle under the skintight faded fabric of her jeans and immediately set himself firm on the saddle.

"You're a better rider than you let on," Denim said to him.

Benjamin replied slyly: "Oh, I'm good at a lot of things. And before I've got to be riding outta Prosperity, I'm hoping to have the opportunity to show you a few."

Denim looked at him appraisingly. "You're purty confident of yourself."

Benjamin spoke honestly. "If I am, Laurie, it's only because I find you about the most attractive girl I've ever seen."

Denim reined back her horse and Benjamin sidled his mount next to her.

"And you've met plenty, I suppose," Denim said playfully.

"Hundreds," Benjamin replied with an elaborate gesture. Then he lifted the brim of his cream-colored Stetson and spoke solemnly. "But none of that matters. Being here with you, admiring you under these wide open skies, with the valley breeze blowin' through your hair—why, I'm resisting every urge just to reach over and kiss you."

"And you keep fightin' that urge, *Mister* Benjamin," Denim said, adopting a manner of mock dignity. Then she smiled her dimpled smile and broke Daybreaker into a run, heading back to Prosperity with her riding companion in swift pursuit.

That night as Ben Straker lay in his bed at the hotel, just down the hall from Denim's room, he found that he could not sleep. The night was hot and the air heavy, but that was not what kept him awake. He couldn't keep his thoughts free of the girl. Every moment that he spent with Denim had filled him with a joy he never could have imagined. But that happiness remained clouded by the knowledge of the task he had been hired to perform. Since she refused to tell him about her purpose for coming into Prosperity—the information demanded by Brock Donovan—he was forced to keep a careful watch on her, anticipating with dread the moment she might ride out to fulfill her promise to kill Donovan. Ben Straker had always been a calm, meticulous thinker, but tonight he was finding it difficult to work out his thoughts with clarity. Even with Denim maintaining a careful emotional distance Ben knew that there was a closeness developing between them. He understood his own feelings, and was overwhelmed with conflict. The more he thought about it, the more convinced he became that he could not carry out Donovan's instructions. He had never welshed on an assignment—it went against his professional code. But he also hadn't reckoned on falling in love with the person he'd been hired to kill.

Finally, toward dawn, he climbed out of bed and began to pace the room. He considered his options, which he knew were limited—and dangerous.

He debated telling Denim about Donovan's bounty on her, asking her to ride away with him, someplace where they could start a new life together. But that would mean revealing the truth about himself—and that was something he simply could not do. Ben also knew that it would not be so easy to back out of his agreement with Donovan. He had already been paid an advance, but money would not be Donovan's primary concern. By failing to complete his end of the bargain, Ben would become in Donovan's fearful eyes a witness to his many crimes. And, as had become Ben's experience in recent months, witnesses past or present were marked as liabilities to Brock Donovan's security.

Liabilities that Donovan had no hesitation about crossing off his books.

Chapter Nine

The Discovery

Brock Donovan enjoyed riding his fringe-topped carriage into town for periodic inspections and to make cash withdrawals from his various enterprises, and was always proud of the respect with which he was invariably greeted. However, since his encounter with the girl called Laurie, he'd stayed clear of Prosperity. While it would have been simple for him to have his sheriff toss her in jail for uttering a threat against his person, he'd decided on a better solution through Ben Straker.

Although town business could wait until Ben took care of this problem, Donovan had another concern that he could not so easily resolve. A question really, that gnawed at his brain relentlessly throughout the long days he had been forced to keep himself safely confined inside his house. . . .

* * *

Marie DuBois was surprised when one of Donovan's hired hands showed up at her room over the saloon and bluntly told her that Brock Donovan wanted her to ride out to his ranch. What puzzled Marie was that Donovan had *never* asked her to visit his house. Since she had become his occasional mistress, Marie would see him only when he came into town, and even then he kept their trysts brief. Maintaining a semblance of secrecy was another matter. Virtually everyone in town knew about their liaisons, which was why Marie DuBois was regarded with a respect uncommon to women in Prosperity.

Because Donovan always left her with a handsome cash gift, Marie was accepting of the impersonal nature of their relationship. But she could not say she felt any kind of love for the man—or even a fleeting affection. While his wants from her were purely physical since his wife could no longer fulfill his needs, Marie too was self-serving, secretly harboring the hope that someday he might permit her to share in his fortune and prestige. Yet it was a desire that she honestly knew would never be. The hard truth was in what George Merrell had said: she had sold herself cheap.

As the carriage that Donovan had provided drove up the pathway to the sprawling white house, Marie again could not suppress her awe. She never imagined that a man of Brock Donovan's crude bearing could live in such a display of splendor. Although she naturally had never been invited to his estate, she occasionally admired it from afar on riding trips she made especially for that purpose.

The driver rode the carriage up to the front steps where he gently pulled on the reins to halt the pair of horses. He then climbed down and stepped round to assist Marie. His awkward attempt at chivalry indicated to Marie that this gesture was an instruction from Brock Donovan, not a politeness of his own choosing.

"Mr. Donovan'll be with you shortly," the man said flatly.

"Should I go inside?" Marie asked.

"Best just to wait out here 'til he comes for you," he said before getting back onto the carriage and riding it away from the house.

Standing alone outside the great house in the quiet of the approaching twilight, Marie suddenly and quite inexplicably experienced an eerie feeling. The house no longer seemed so impressive to her. Up close it took on a foreboding, almost tragic air that she could not define, but that she could definitely absorb. Looking out into the great expanse of land that Donovan owned, she could detect no activity and felt isolated . . . and vulnerable.

After a while the front door to the house opened and Brock Donovan presented himself. He responded icily to her feeble attempt at a smile. Instead, with a quick jerk of his head, he motioned for her to come inside.

Marie lifted the hem of her long, lace-frilled dress as she negotiated the steps. By the time she reached the open doorway, Donovan had disappeared and once again she felt alone and uneasy.

She walked into the entrance hall. The house was like a cavern, yet there was no sign of Donovan. She debated whether she should stay put or perhaps proceed inside.

Donovan suddenly reappeared from the parlor. He was looking at her with a stern expression, the lines in his heavy face pronounced. As he stood in the entraceway to the room he said nothing. But words were not necessary as Marie suspected why he had sent for her. Only she did not understand why he had wanted her to come out to his house.

But then she understood little of what went on inside the mind of Brock Donovan.

He gestured for her to come into the parlor. She obeyed.

The heavy curtain overlooking the front property was drawn and the room was encased in a gloomy atmosphere.

Marie took a seat on the sofa but Donovan remained standing, clearly relishing his position of authority, of looking down at people for whom he had little respect. Marie understood she was in that category. He was holding a glass of bourbon but did not offer Marie a drink.

"Word's come to me that you've struck up a friendship with that girl stranger," Donovan said brusquely.

Marie replied tentatively. "I've spoken to her a few times."

Donovan's face became even more hardened. "Heard more'n that. Heard you two have gotten to be real close."

Marie did not understand what he was getting at. But suddenly she felt apprehensive.

"She's just a girl, Brock," she explained. "Someone I've sort of taken a liking to."

"What's she been tellin' you?" Donovan demanded.

"We just talk . . . girl talk," Marie answered.

Donovan was quickly losing patience. "I'm askin' you a question, Marie, and I expect a straight answer. What's she doin' in town?"

Marie struggled to keep her nervousness in check. "I don't know, Brock. Honest, I don't. I asked her a couple of times, but she won't say."

Donovan eyed her flatly for several moments, as if seeking a crack in her attempt at sincerity. "Well, I want you to do somethin' for me, Marie. I want you to find that girl and I want you to tell her that Mr. Donovan told *you* what she came to town for. I reckon once she thinks *you* know, then maybe she'll have more to say to you."

"But I told you, I don't know why she's—" Marie began to say.

Donovan spoke abruptly. "She don't know that, Marie. That's the point." He pulled a ten-dollar bill out of his pocket, crumpled it, and tossed it almost contemptuously onto the sofa next to Marie.

Donovan gave her a final instruction. "You be back here tomorrow with what I wanta know. Understand? I'll get Luke to take you back to town."

When Marie's head began to clear she felt even more anxious. The pieces of a nefarious puzzle were beginning to fit together. Yet there was one important piece missing, and Marie could not guess what that was. Still, she was worried. She saw plainly that whatever the reason Denim had come into Prosperity had Donovan concerned. But she could not understand why a man of Brock Donovan's position and power would be so troubled by it.

Marie was determined to find out the truth from Denim—if only perhaps to save her life.

The next morning Marie walked into the hotel restaurant and found Denim having breakfast with a male companion.

Marie knew of course that Denim had been spending time with the young stranger. Consequently, she and the girl hadn't spoke much over the last couple of days. While initially approving and encouraging of their friendship, Marie's talk with Brock Donovan aroused in her a suspicion of anyone showing even a passing interest in the girl.

Denim was delighted to see Marie and quickly introduced her to "Benjamin": Walter Benjamin—or simply Ben. The young man rose politely from his chair and invited Marie to join them for a cup of coffee. Marie accepted. But Denim could tell immediately that something was bothering her friend.

Benjamin was amiable and talked freely, though Denim began to feel a little uncomfortable by the many questions Marie asked him: where he was from, his line of work, his reason for being in Prosperity. It was as if she were interrogating him.

Yet Benjamin answered all of her questions easily and without appearing offended—and was convincing in his replies. He was polite, charming, and well-spoken, but Marie inexplicably sensed something troubling about the man.

After breakfast, Benjamin and Denim prepared to walk over to the livery stable to get their horses for their morning ride. Marie wanted to hold Denim back and somehow find a way to talk to her, alone. But her head was so muddled she could not come up with any convincing lie with which to stall her.

Despite her independence, Denim was a naive girl. Trusting. She would have a difficult time understanding Marie's concern. Marie also had her own guilt. She felt responsible for encouraging Denim's friendship with the stranger—and she was fearful that her good intentions might have serious consequences.

Before Denim and Benjamin could leave the restaurant, Marie said to the girl: "Denim . . . be careful."

Denim instantly detected the odd tone in Marie's voice and regarded her quizzically.

Marie then flicked a glance toward Benjamin. In just that quick second when their eyes met, Marie chilled with the realization that her fears may well be justified.

"You don't have to worry, Miss DuBois," Benjamin said to her, his voice easy but with a hard glint in his eye. "Laurie is one girl who knows how to take care of herself."

Marie watched them go. She would wait for the girl to come back. And then she would find the proper words to tell her about Brock Donovan. She prayed that until that time the girl would be safe.

Maurice, the restaurant manager, watched the couple leave as well. Once they were gone he walked over and stood next to Marie. He looked nervous and his brow was perspiring. He pulled out a cloth and dabbed the beads of moisture from his forehead.

"I declare, I never expected to see *that* man in Prosperity," he said in a quavering voice.

Marie gave him a puzzled look.

"And that . . . that *girl,*" he added with a sweep of his hand. He turned to Marie, saw her uncomprehending expression, and added hastily: "She's a friend of yours. Surely you must know that man she's been keeping company with is Ben Straker."

The color suddenly drained from Marie's face. "Ben Straker . . . ," she said in a whisper.

"Yes," Maurice said, vigorously nodding his head. "I recognized him immediately from my time in San Francisco. Oh, he's a man you want to stay clear of. They say he's killed more men than the Apaches."

The statement, of course, was an exaggeration based on the campfire legends so prevalent in the West—but such was the reputation of the infamous gunman.

"I didn't know . . . I couldn't have known," Marie muttered.

"If he's come to Prosperity, Miss DuBois, it can only be for one thing." Maurice started perspiring again and wiped off the sweat.

Marie spoke urgently, "I'll need a buggy from the livery stable, Maurice. It's important that I see someome right away."

"Certainly," Maurice said in an equally quick voice. "I'll send someone to fetch it for you immediately."

Denim and Benjamin enjoyed a beautiful ride that morning. The air was crisp and invigorating. Both felt refreshed as they galloped through their usual grasslands trail, eventually veering off into the high plains that led them deep into the pristine valley, far from the town. Off in the distance stood Brock Donovan's impressive ranch. Benjamin brought his mount to a halt and Denim rode up beside him. Benjamin gave the girl a subtle glance, hoping to gauge a reaction.

Her eyes swept over the spread with an expression that revealed nothing. Nor did she speak.

"The fellow who lives there owns practically the entire valley," Benjamin said.

"Must be an important man," Denim returned neutrally.

"He is. Name's Brock Donovan."

Denim nodded noncommitally and waited a bit before asking: "How'd he come by all this?"

Benjamin pulled up on his saddle. "He's a shrewd man. Some might even call him ruthless."

Denim's eyes sparked as she turned to her companion. "You know him?"

"Know of him," Benjamin lied smoothly. "Hard not to know of Brock Donovan in these parts." He paused for a moment, then went on, "He's made a lot of enemies in his dealings. Some, I've heard, have tried to even the score. That's why he keeps himself protected."

Denim sat silent on her mount.

"That's a fool's way," Benjamin said. He added with a sudden emphasis: "Hard to kill a man like Donovan."

Denim's expression was vaguely thoughtful. She remained quiet, then finally breathed softly and gazed over her shoulder at the trail behind them.

"Reckon we should be headin' back," she said.

Benjamin was not quite ready. "Laurie . . . ," he started to say before stopping himself.

The girl, though, was curious, if only by the sudden odd tone of his voice. "What d'you want to be tellin' me?" she asked.

Benjamin collected himself and finally spoke the words he had been rehearsing in his mind all morning. "I'm going to be riding out soon, probably tomorrow. I'd like it if you might come with me."

Denim looked a little sad. "I can't," she said. "I gotta be ridin' back to Caillou. Ain't seen my grandpa . . . seems like forever."

Benjamin's expression did not change, though his weight shifted slightly on the saddle.

"Aim to be headin' back in a day or two," Denim added, raising her Stetson so that a bundle of blond hair fell freely across her face. She brushed it to the side. "Reckon we'll be travelin' in opposite directions."

"Is that your plan, Laurie—to stay in Caillou?" Benjamin asked gently.

"Don't know for certain," Denim replied with a lift of her shoulder. "It's just my grandpa and me . . . and he ain't been well. Though he won't admit it. Ain't been easy leavin' him when I go on tour. He kinda depends on me."

"And you . . . depend on him?" Benjamin said.

"He's the only family that I got," Denim replied simply.

"Laurie . . . I don't want to be leaving you," Benjamin finally said.

Denim's blue eyes grew soft as she looked at Benjamin.

Ben Straker was in many ways a cold, conscienceless human being, but he chilled at the thought of how Denim would react when she returned to Caillou. To find her grandfather dead many days with a bullet in the back of his skull. And he, Ben Straker, had been the one to kill him. That fact was one Ben knew she would never have to know. But "Benjamin" would need to be there for her.

"Let me ride back with you," he suggested.

"But you got your own work to do," Denim argued. "You can't be givin' that up just to ride back with me to a dirt farm."

Benjamin smiled. "My work . . . doesn't seem that important anymore, now that I've found you. I know what I feel, Laurie, and it's strong. I'm hoping that it might be what you're feeling too."

Denim took a long while before she answered.

"Reckon it is," she finally said, meekly. "But . . . it sure ain't what I was lookin' for."

"Don't fight it, Laurie," Benjamin urged.

Benjamin pulled his mare abreast of Denim. And for the first time he touched her, gently taking her hand. She did not resist. Instead she welcomed the feel of his skin against hers, which was smooth and not hardened by a rough life on the range.

"Being from the East, I don't know much about farming," Benjamin confessed. "But sounds to me like you'll be needing help—" He hesitated. "If your grandpa is ill."

"I can't be askin' you to do that."

"You're not," Benjamin said with a gentle smile.

Denim returned the smile, delicately. But she became quiet as she patted Daybreaker forward.

They were both silent with their thoughts on the slow ride back to Prosperity. Only briefly did Benjamin consider the consequences of his betraying Brock Donovan. But he was a man who had lived much of his life not acknowledging fear. He determined that not even the threat of Donovan would deter him from leaving the valley—with Denim.

And Denim too had made a decision. Tomorrow would be the day. She would not wait out the week. Nor *could* she. What she had dreaded since first meeting Benjamin had happened. She had discovered a side of herself that she had never really explored. A vulnerability that she had never before recognized—or even considered that she might possess. One that she hardly knew how to acknowledge. She didn't embrace this new discovery of herself. Rather, she resented it, saw it almost as a weakness that would surely work against her in fulfilling the obligation she owed her parents. What was most important in completing her task was that her heart must remain hardened. She could not allow herself to lose sight of what she had determined for years she must do. But what filled her with apprehension was that she believed it might already be too late. She had allowed herself the intrusion of affection. Maybe it was even more than that, though that was a possibility she was not ready to wholly accept. And so she made the decision that *tomorrow* she would meet with Brock Donovan and settle all accounts. Otherwise, she might not be able to hold on to the hate that had brought her to this day of reckoning. Tomorrow . . . before sunset . . . before riding back to Caillou—with Benjamin . . . Brock Donovan would be dead.

The buggy raced along the rolling valley road, Marie barely maintaining control of the reins as she whipped the horse into a dead run. In the distance stood Brock Donovan's house.

Marie did not have to hear the truth from Denim—of why she had come to Prosperity. Her only concern was why Brock Donovan had brought in a professional gunman, evidently with the intention to kill her young friend. The thoughts that flooded her brain filled her with such dread, such disgust, that she gave no mind to her own well-being once she confronted Donovan. She knew he was a man not to be challenged—especially by a woman. Marie suppressed a shudder as she faced the truth that because of how she sold herself she was even *less* than a woman in Donovan's eyes.

Donovan had heard the buggy approach from inside the house and he pushed his imposing bulk onto the veranda and watched its frantic approach. Two of his workmen were spurring their mounts into rapid springing gaits behind the buggy, prepared to defend their boss against this intruder. Donovan himself swallowed a heavy breath as he readied himself for what he had been expecting. The girl had returned to kill him. Silently he cursed Ben Straker for failing in his duty and made a vow to deal with his incompetency after he took care of the girl. He walked back into his house to retrieve his mounted .45 Sharpe rifle, a Civil War trophy prized by marksmen and buffalo hunters because of its great range. Damn fool girl, he thought almost pitifully as he levered a single round into the breech. Donovan had never used the weapon to kill a man, but he was an accomplished shot. The girl was riding right into a bullet. She would be dead before she had the chance to climb out of the buggy.

Donovan moved back to the main door of the house. He peered through the side glass to make sure the girl wasn't standing at the ready, waiting for him to step outside to ambush him. What he saw instead made him drop the rifle to his side.

It was Marie—apparently come to report her findings.

Brock Donovan was a supremely egotistical and self-centered man. It never occurred to him that her urgency could be for any other reason than to accommodate his demand. He laid his rifle aside and went outside before his men could intercept her.

"Leave her be," Donovan commanded the two range workers as they hurriedly dismounted once they pulled abreast of the buggy. He then gestured with a rough sweep of his arm for Marie to follow him inside the house.

Marie glared at the two riders before she maneuvered herself down from her seat and moved as quickly as she could up the steps to the house. Donovan waited for her at the door.

Once inside, Marie could no longer contain her outrage. She dared to slap Donovan across his face. "You cowardly, no-good . . . !" she spat.

Donovan's features registered shock at the unprovoked assault. Then his face became flushed, contorting with a sudden fury. He grabbed Marie tightly by the wrists, forcing her arms upward.

Marie grimaced in pain under his strength, though she remained firm in her resolve and instantly plunged into her accusation.

Her voice trembled. "You brought in Ben Straker to kill that girl! What kind of man are you?"

Donovan's angry features gradually relaxed. "You figgered it out, huh? Or maybe you was talkin' to someone. Straker, for instance."

"I've never met the man," Marie lied. "But I know he's in town."

Donovan let go of her wrists. "Maybe you're smarter than I give you credit for, Marie." He turned and took a few steps forward. When he next spoke, his voice was muted. "I gave that girl no provocation. Yet she rides out to my house threatenin' to kill me."

"She's just a child, Brock," Marie argued. "She can't do you any harm."

Donovan spoke with emphasis. "From what I hear, I got plenty to be worried 'bout. Just 'cause she's young and a girl don't mean I can take her threat lightly."

Marie sighed. "Why in heaven would she want to see you dead?"

"That's what I was aimin' to have you find out," Donovan said thickly.

"She hasn't told me a thing," Marie insisted. "But if what you're saying is true, she must have a good reason."

Donovan shrugged. For a moment he became contemplative. "Sometimes when a man builds success the way I have, people get insulted."

Marie could not accept such an offhand reply. "That girl went through a lot to ride up here. Too much to make a claim against your life for a mere insult."

"I suspect you didn't make much of an effort to find out what I asked you to," Donovan said.

Marie took a bold stance. "I found out all I needed. The truth about the kind of man you are, Brock."

"Takin' sides, Marie," Donovan said darkly. "I wouldn't advise it."

Marie refused to be intimidated, despite Donovan's unsubtle threat. "If you think I'm just gonna stand by while your hired killer—"

Donovan cut her off. Both his words and his tone allowed for no further argument. "One of us gotta die, Marie. And I think you know I'm a man committed to self-preservation."

"You're a coward!" Marie returned.

Donovan penetrated Marie with his piercing stare. "I'm givin' you the advice I gave that girl. Don't try to interfere."

Marie returned to town, feeling helpless and afraid. Denim had already stabled Daybreaker and was waiting for her inside the lobby of the Prosperity Hotel.

Marie was relieved to see that no harm had come to the girl. But she did not know what she could do to offer her further protection. As long as Denim stayed in town she was destined for trouble. As was Marie. Donovan had assured her that "eyes in the town" would be watching and that any attempt by Marie to help the girl would be reported to him—and the consequences would not be pleasant. Marie knew that this was no idle threat. Donovan only had to give the order and she would be removed from his life forever. It was something Marie had considered before: when she was no longer of use to him.

No matter how much Marie cared for Denim, regardless of the cherished memories the girl evoked in her, Marie doubted that she truly possessed the courage to defy Brock Donovan.

Denim was eager to speak with her. Marie tried to keep her concerns in check; she did not want to let on that she knew more than she had ever wanted to know. To manage this, she would have to somehow summon those marginal skills she had learned as an actress. But she doubted she was up to the task.

Denim's face was aglow, her dimples pronounced, yet her tone was subdued. "I been thinkin' it over, Marie, and you're right. I gotta start thinkin' 'bout makin' a life for myself."

Marie felt her heart start to race.

"After tomorrow I'll be headin' back to Caillou," Denim told her. "And this time I'll be stayin'. Work with my grandpa on the farm." Her long-lashed eyelids lowered and her voice became even more quiet. "And Benjamin says he wants to come with me."

With a great effort, Marie managed to keep herself composed.

Denim's voice perked up. "Ain't that funny? He's a city slicker and he wants to work with me on the farm doin' chores."

Marie wished there was some way she could spare Denim the truth. But now there was no keeping it from her. She feared the consequences would be unpleasant and would probably affect the friendship the two had formed. But Marie owed it to the girl to be honest with her.

She suddenly felt weak and dizzy, almost faint, and clasped onto Denim's forearm for support. The girl put her arm around Marie and guided her over to the sofa near the draped entrance that led into the restaurant. Marie noticed Maurice watching them from the kitchen, his ferretlike features creased into an expression of concern.

"You're sick agin, ain't you?" Denim said as she helped settle Marie into a chair.

Marie's face looked bloodless. Her breathing was short. She waited until she had regained herself before speaking the words she did not want to say.

"Denim, you've got to know the last thing I'd ever want to do is hurt you. But it's because of how I care for you that I need to tell you this."

Denim looked at her, suddenly apprehensive by the seriousness of Marie's attitude.

Before Marie could continue Maurice walked over carrying a glass of water, which he handed to Marie. His concern was solely for the woman; he did not even acknowledge Denim, whom he saw only as a troublemaker, and who he blamed for Marie's sudden distress. Marie sipped from the glass and stopped herself from asking for something a little more potent. She returned the glass to Maurice along with a look that told him she would be all right.

Once Maurice returned to the kitchen, but keeping himself within earshot of their conversation, Marie said to Denim: "This isn't the place for us to talk."

"We can go upstairs to my room," the girl suggested.

Marie nodded. She tried to rise, but was still weak. Denim quickly helped her to her feet and together they walked up the staircase to the girl's room.

Once inside with the door locked behind them, Marie immediately laid down on the bed and propped herself up on the pillow. It was a small room, cramped rather than cozy, with much of the space taken up by the bed, a side table, and a writing desk and chair. The heavy curtain over the window filtered out much of the sunlight and the room was dark and had a musty smell.

Denim asked Marie if she could get her anything, but Marie declined. Her face looked pained and more deeply embedded with lines. She patted the mattress, inviting the girl to sit next to her on the bed. Denim sat and said gently: "You sure took ill sudden."

Marie did not acknowledge her concern. She sucked in a breath that rattled deep inside her damaged lungs. "Denim," she said carefully, "I've gotta tell you something." She took a steadying breath. "Something you don't want to know."

Denim crinkled her forehead.

"It's about that fella," Marie said.

"Benjamin?" Denim said with a curious tilt of her head.

Marie gave her head a slight rock. Her voice was strange. "That's the name he wants you to know him by. But he's not Walter Benjamin, as he calls himself."

"I don't know what you mean," Denim said cautiously.

Marie spoke forthright. "Denim, have you ever heard of Ben Straker?"

"I . . . think I heard of him," Denim replied tentatively.

"He's a hired gun. A killer," Marie said.

Denim's expression was puzzled. She honestly couldn't see what any of this had to do with her.

"Denim . . . that man who calls himself Walter Benjamin *is* Ben Straker."

Denim practically leaped from the side of the bed. “That ain’t so!” she exclaimed.

Marie kept her voice calm. “Denim, please—please just sit down and let me explain—”

But Denim would not listen to such an outrageous accusation.

“I don’t know why you’re tellin’ me this, Marie, but Benjamin ain’t no killer,” Denim said in protest.

“Don’t you think I want to believe that?” Marie said sympathetically. “But he was recognized. And Denim, as hard as I know this is for you to accept, feeling as you do toward him, I would never lie to you.”

“No, it jus’ ain’t so,” Denim replied, shaking her head vigorously as if to physically keep out Marie’s words.

“Denim—”

“You’re a liar,” the girl spat with venom.

“Denim, sit down,” Marie said sternly.

The girl calmed herself a bit. Then she regarded Marie with a look of stubborn defiance. But when she realized that Marie was not going to back down, she reluctantly sat herself on the bed, though not close to the woman.

Marie collected herself before she offered another truth she’d kept from the girl. But now it was vital that she reveal it.

“I never told you why you’re special to me, Laurie,” she said softly. “Why I took such an instant liking to you. Well . . . it’s because . . . I had a daughter who, if she were alive, would be about your age. And you remind me so much of her. Of how she'd be today." Her eyes began to tear. "The way you look . . . and your plain stubborn ways, just as she was. Born with an independence that blinds you to all reason. Nobody was happier than me when I thought you'd found the right kind of fella. And as much as this hurts you, it breaks my heart every bit as much."

"You don't care nothin' 'bout my feelin's, Marie," Denim stated sourly.

"You're wrong."

Denim swallowed. "What he feels toward me, I ain't ever known before."

"Love, honey?" Marie said. "I assure you, a man like Ben Straker could never know love."

"Maybe it's *you* that's never known love," Denim returned belligerently.

Denim instantly regretted her words, spoken in haste. But her emotion was genuine. Benjamin was no gunman. Why was Marie, who was supposed to be her friend, lying to her?

The girl huffed, then got up and started for the door. Marie called after her: "Denim, don't!"

The soft innocence of Denim's face had suddenly hardened into an expression of determined maturity. Her voice was firm. "If what you're tellin' me is true—*an' it ain't*—I gotta find out for myself."

Denim slammed the door behind her as she left the room and walked quickly down the corridor. She did not know if Benjamin was in his room, but she knocked hard against the door before impatiently turning the knob. The door was unlocked. She quickly pushed the door opened and stepped inside.

She found Benjamin standing by the open curtain of his window, his slight physique silhouetted against the bright afternoon sun. He had his coat off and wore a vest over his striped shirt.

He started, as if interrupted from deep thought, halting his quick reflex to reach for the gun lying exposed on the bedside table.

"Laurie," he said, surprised.

Denim closed the door behind her. Benjamin could see that her face was troubled. He walked toward her. He noticed that her eyes were searching.

Denim took a deliberate step forward and spoke to the point. "I gotta know if what I heard is true."

Benjamin put out his hand. Denim resisted taking it. Not until she knew the absolute truth. From Benjamin himself.

She spoke solidly. "If you look me straight in the eye and tell me it ain't so . . . I'll believe you."

Benjamin looked at her, innocently. "All you have to do is ask," he said.

But Ben Straker turned cold as he already expected what was coming. He'd been preparing for the possibility of this moment.

Denim straightened her posture and spoke her question. "Are you Ben Straker?"

Benjamin did not hesitate. Not a muscle in his face

betrayed what he was about to answer. He gazed into her eyes and said simply: "No."

The room went silent. The tenseness that had taken hold of Denim gradually eased from her body. But her eyes remained locked on Benjamin's, whose own focus did not waver. She carefully studied those eyes . . . and she believed him. Her grandpa had told her years before that a person's eyes could never hide deceit. But she could not have known that Ben Straker had many years of practice.

Again Benjamin put out his hand. Denim felt she could now accept his touch and she slid her long, slender fingers into his palm. She moved her body forward, gently, tentatively, and Benjamin drew her close. He kissed her, and Denim responded. But then she pulled back. There was still a question that troubled her.

"Then why would Marie be sayin' such a thing?" Denim said sadly.

"Marie?" Benjamin said with surprise.

Denim nodded. "It was she who told me you was Straker."

Ben Straker never would have suspected the woman, even though he remembered how she regarded him with more than a little suspicion when they had met in the hotel dining room that morning. All of those questions . . . probing him. But he didn't know her, had never met her before. How could she have known about him? Who he was . . .

"I can't start to guess her reason." Benjamin sighed. "And it's really not important. As long as *you* trust me."

"I knew she was wrong," Denim replied softly, gratefully.

They stood in each other's embrace for a long while.

Benjamin whispered with affection: "It's our life, Laurie. Our sharing."

Denim nuzzled her head into his shoulder.

Benjamin gently assured her. "I promise that I'll always be with you, Laurie."

He sat them both on the edge of the bed and tenderly pulled her closer. He whispered: "I love you, Laurie."

Denim wanted to echo his words. She imagined how they would feel leaving her lips. But she held back, unsure of speaking words she had never said—not even to her grandpa, the man she loved most in the world. To prevent herself from looking into Benjamin's eyes she turned her head to the side, toward the night table. . . . .

Where a reflection instantly caught her eye. A glint of gold.

Denim's whole body instantly stiffened as she recognized the pocket watch . . . that she had presented as a gift to her grandfather.

Her breath lodged in her throat, and when she turned to face Benjamin, her eyes were wide and her face pale, drained of color.

"That watch belonged to my grandpa," she said numbly.

Denim pulled herself away from Benjamin's embrace and scooped up the watch from the night table. With a palpitating heart, she snapped open the cover, hoping the vainest hope that what she expected to find inside would not be there.

But it was—the picture of herself. She closed the cover and pressed it tightly against her chest. Although her expression was pained, she struggled to control her emotions.

Ben Straker's own features were rigid; there was nothing he could think of to say. There were no words to explain. The truth he had wanted so desperately to keep from her was revealed.

Denim pulled herself from the bed and stepped away from Ben. Her voice trembled as she said: "The only way you coulda got this is by takin' it from him."

Ben lowered his eyes. He did not even attempt to speak.

Denim looked straight at him, the softness gone from her eyes, her gaze now cold and condemning. "Then it is true: You *are* Ben Straker! A killer."

"Who I *was*, Laurie," Ben weakly tried to explain.

"No. You're not just a killer, but a *murderer*!" Denim spat. "And you"—she could barely speak the words—"murdered my grandpa."

Although Ben knew there was nothing he could say to defend himself, he muttered: "I was hired to do a job. I couldn't have known . . ."

"Hired!" Denim erupted. "By who? Donovan?" She spoke tearfully. "He was the finest man that ever lived. You tried to make me believe you . . . and all them lies. And why're you here now, Ben Straker? To kill me? Is that why you stole my grandpa's watch? So you had a picture with you of who you was gonna kill."

"I could never hurt you, Laurie," Ben responded.

"You knew all along who I was," Denim said.

Ben didn't acknowledge.

Denim stiffened her pose. "And you also know why I come here."

Ben swallowed. "Laurie, you don't know what you're up against," he warned. "I want to protect you."

"I ain't afraid of Brock Donovan and I ain't of you, Ben Straker," Denim said with defiance. "But you'd best be a-feared of me. 'Cause 'fore I ride outta Prosperity, there'll be two notches on my gun belt."

Denim began backing toward the door, cautiously, still penetrating Ben with her cold stare. A look that expressed a hatred such as Ben had never seen.

"I won't be givin' you the chance to shoot me in the back," Denim said with a sneer.

But Ben didn't even try to stop her. He remained seated on the bed as he watched the back-stepping girl finally reach the door and then slam out of the room. He sat in the oppressive quiet of his room for a long time—not moving, barely breathing. He knew he had lost her. He also knew that his one hope of leaving the bloody life of Ben Straker was forever behind him . . . and that there was no longer anything personal to keep him from carrying out Brock Donovan's instructions.

Denim had held herself together, but it was all just a facade. If she'd given vent to her true emotions either she or Ben Straker would now be lying dead. Probably her . . . because she had not expected to learn what she had and certainly had not prepared herself the way she had all those years for her showdown with Donovan. Worse, she had been made vulnerable. She felt that she could have loved "Benjamin." He was the man with whom she could have envisioned a future and a fine life together. But now he too would have to pay for what he had done. He had betrayed her just as Brock Donovan had betrayed her parents. And now her beloved grandpa—killed by Straker most surely on Donovan's instructions. Both men had taken Denim's family from her. For that there could be no forgiveness. Only an obligation. . . . .

Denim could not bring herself to go back to her room to confess to Marie that the woman had been right. Her hurt was too great and she had to be alone. Instead she left the hotel and proceeded to the livery stable. She needed the closeness of her horse, who loved her unconditionally and on whom she could always depend. She pressed her face against Daybreaker's cheek and allowed herself a moment to sob while the horse remained patient and still. Gradually Denim recovered, and as she wiped the dampness of her tears from her eyes she smiled proudly at her horse.

"You're always there for me, ain't you, fella?"

Daybreaker snorted.

"All we got now is each other," she sighed. "An' if'n you give me your word likewise, I promise you that we'll never be without each other."

Daybreaker neighed and stamped a front hoof on the stable floor.

Denim couldn't help but grin at the animal's 'acknowledgment.' "You're a smart horse, Daybreaker."

The girl tossed her saddle over Daybreaker and rode out hard and fast into the valley, unaware that both Marie and Ben were watching her from their respective hotel windows, each absorbed with their own thoughts. Marie knew with sadness that Denim had indeed discovered the truth. Ben debated whether he could really bring himself to kill the girl he had wanted to love.

Escaping the now-stifling confines of Prosperity, Denim was thankful for the refeshing breeze that caressed her face and whistled cool gusts through her long hair. She continued to ride until she was some miles away, where she was surrounded only by the clean color of the land, away from the lies and greed and hypocrisies of a so-called civilized society that she had never truly been able to embrace—or that had accepted her for being who she was.

She brought Daybreaker to a halt. And then she swung off the horse, walked a few paces, and finally gave full vent to her anger and sorrow. She broke down completely. And that was what she wanted. What she needed to do. Just drain herself completely of those conflicting emotions that might once more make her vulnerable. Again Daybreaker stood nearby patiently, as if he understood.

Denim had rarely cried in her life and so much of what had been pent-up inside her through the years was suddenly and strongly released. But mainly it was for her grandpa . . . and the man who killed him. She alternately cried and screamed, letting her voice echo through the still valley. And finally, her emotions spent, she dropped to her knees in the tall grass and slowly reclaimed herself.

Reclaimed *Denim* Ryder.

It was dark when Denim rode back into town. Old Tom Becker was not at the stable when she rode out, but he was inside tending to some work when she returned. She was subdued as she walked past him and led Daybreaker back to his stall and Tom could tell that something was wrong. Since they'd become friendly, Denim had always been a talkative girl with him. Tom debated offering an ear if she had a mind to talk about whatever seemed to be troubling her. But he decided against it as he got the distinct feeling that the girl preferred to be alone. And Tom Becker managed to convince himself that he was *not* a meddler.

Denim walked by him on the way out. " 'Night" was all she said. Tom replied with a nod that she never even looked back to see.

Denim decided to move her few belongings out of the hotel room and maybe come back a little later and bed down next to Daybreaker in the stable. It would be her last night in Prosperity, and she was eager to move on. Tomorrow she would see through her promise to Brock Donovan . . . and maybe Ben Straker, then be on her way. But to where? She didn't know. She could not imagine going back to Caillou without her grandpa being there.

But where else could she go? Maybe . . . she no longer needed a real home. Just keep riding with Daybreaker and camp out under the stars. A life of solitude. The thought seemed mighty appealing to her. She never again wanted to grow close to another human being.

She walked along the boardwalk back to the hotel. She could hear the music and laughter emanating from the Golden Circle Saloon. But other than that the streets were quiet. She looked across the road and saw Sheriff Tom Brough watching her as he sucked on his pipe while taking in a little night air. It was a crisp, cloudless night, like a canvas hanging over the valley, pinpricked with thousands of distant stars.

She entered the empty lobby of the hotel and proceeded up the staircase. She moved quietly. She did not want to chance running into Ben. Not yet. That moment was still to come. Nor did she particularly want to see Marie, whom she hoped had long since vacated her room.

But the door to her room was unlocked, which meant that Marie might still be inside. If so, Denim hoped that she was fast asleep. There was nothing she felt she could explain to her. Nor did she want to.

Then—she halted as a chill swept through her. What if . . . it wasn't Marie? What if . . . it was Ben Straker? Waiting for her. Wanting either to talk with her . . . or kill her? But no, she quickly thought. Ben would never be so careless as to alert her by leaving the door unlocked. He was too clever. He was a professional killer. Still, she instinctively reached for the .45 Colt in her gun belt while her free hand twisted the doorknob. She carefully ventured inside the room. It was dark, but immediately she noticed that the bedside table lantern was on, emanating a muted glow. *She* had not lit the lantern. Someone else had. Someone who might still be inside the room. She clicked back the hammer on her revolver.

"All right. I know someone's—" she began to say.

She heard a quick shuffling off to the side. As she started to turn there was another noise directly behind her. She never had time to react as something powerful gripped her around the throat and her brief struggle ceased when she was struck by a heavy blow against the back of her head that sent her sprawling to the floor. She held onto consciousness only for an instant before she was absorbed into the blackness of a deep, dreamless sleep.

She wished she could have stayed asleep. Safe in her cocoon of peace and darkness. Because as she slowly and groggily awoke to a harsh spray of liquor being spit-sprayed onto her face by a blurry figure she could not identify, Denim felt as if the back of her head had been caved in. The pain was crippling. Hurting so much she didn't know where she was . . . or even who she was.

The voices that surrounded her were likewise vague. Vague . . . but threatening.

"She's finally comin' around, Brett," someone giggled.

"You hit her pretty hard. Didn't think she'd ever wake up."

"Mebbe better for her if she didn't," the man named

Brett growled as he raised himself off of the girl. He wiped his mouth and said with disgust: "Hell, all I'm doin' is wastin' good whiskey."

More voices . . . coming at the semiconscious Denim from all directions.

"She still ain't with us. Lemme slap her awake."

"No more hittin'. Hit her agin an' we *will* kill her. And that ain't the way Mr. Donovan wants it."

"Dead is dead."

"That *ain't* the way he wants it done."

"Well, just let's get on with it."

"You in a hurry to watch a woman die, Curt? Mr. Donovan gave us specific instructions. He wants her to be fully aware of what's gonna happen to her." The voice rose to an angry pitch: "She look 'fully aware' to you, Curt?"

Denim felt herself being jerked up and dragged roughly across the floor, finally being deposited equally roughly onto a chair. She struggled to bring herself around so that she could understand what was happening. But all she could really discern was that her head hurt something awful and that she had a difficult time focusing her vision on the shadowy forms grouped around her in the dimly lit room.

"Still say you hit her too hard. She won't come outta it 'til a week Tuesday."

Denim's head began to loll as she once more started to slip into unconsciousness.

Then she felt oily fingers press into her cheeks and her head being jerked upward. The face that met hers was sallow, thin, and hawklike—and vulture mean. It was Ned Randolph, Brock Donovan's ramrodder, the brute who had earlier had a run-in at the saloon with George Merrell.

"Not so fast," Ned said. He spoke close to her face and Denim noted that his breath was redolent of tobacco and cheap rotgut whiskey. "You ain't goin' back to no sweet dreams." He turned to the others as he kept his fingers embedded in the girl's cheeks. "Hey, boys, ain't never felt skin this girly soft. Soft 'n' purty. But dresses like a cowpuncher. How d'ya figger that?"

The tight grip of his fingers relaxed and a calloused palm stinking of tobacco began a slow rise and descent along the side of Denim's face. The girl waited until the hand crossed her mouth—and then she snapped open her jaws and bit down hard on the side of his hand, holding fast and drawing blood.

Ned howled in agony, sounding like an injured child, and tried to twist his hand free. Denim just clamped down tighter.

"Get her offa me!" Ned bellowed.

But instead of coming to his aid, the others in the room doubled over in laughter, infuriating the cowboy.

"*Get her off, dammit!*" Ned cried again.

"If she don't let loose, might have to cut your hand off, Ned," one of the men whooped.

Ned hastened to withdraw his six-shooter with his free hand and lodge the barrel against the side of Denim's head. "I'll blow you to kingdom come!" he swore.

Denim felt a sharp blow against the back of her head,

which drew her bottom jaw slack. Ned backed away, fairly whimpering.

The man who had hit Denim with the butt end of his gun was named Henderson. He'd slugged her just hard enough to daze her, not knock her out. He said directly to Ned: "Ain't no one here killin' no one. And keep your voice down, you idiot, 'fore you wake everyone in the hotel."

"Looka what she done to my hand!" Ned said, stupidly pressing the fingers of his other hand under the wound so that a gout of blood spurted forth.

"Wrap a kerchief 'round it 'fore you bleed to death," Henderson said with disgust. "You're takin' it worse than girly here."

"Yeh, sure," Ned said, grimacing. But first, in a sudden move, he gave a hard kick to the chair, sending Denim crashing to the floor. Ned then drew back his foot and prepared to kick her in the belly.

Henderson pulled him back by the collar of his shirt. "I said go clean up," he repeated firmly.

Ned nodded his head vigorously. But he was not about to forget his humiliation. "It's gonna be a real pleasure watchin' *you* die," he hissed at Denim.

Henderson looked down at Denim's moaning, semiconscious form curled on the floor. "You made a fool's move comin' into Prosperity," he said to her in an almost gentle tone. "You made a bigger mistake tryin' to go agin Brock Donovan." He turned away from her but continued talking. "Fact is, you ain't leavin' town alive."

Denim attempted to lift herself on an elbow. She was starting to revive more fully.

"We can do it quick . . . or we can make it slow," Henderson added. "You make the choice."

Denim's eyes were locked tight on Henderson. She inched her left hand slowly toward her gun belt, her fingers sliding past the waistband of her jeans.

Henderson smiled sadly as one of the cowboys lifted Denim's leather-fringed gun belt high in the air and waved it. Henderson said: "None of these boys is the brightest star in the sky, but now you're plain insultin' us."

Denim turned her head aside as another big-bellied man smacked his fat wet lips in a mockery of a kiss.

Henderson sighed. "Tell us why you've come to kill Mr. Donovan and I give you my word we'll go easy on you. Otherwise . . ."

Denim managed a weak smile. "Took five of you, did it? You're all as much cowards as your boss." She lifted herself higher and spoke in proud defiance. "I won't be tellin' you *nothin'*."

Henderson's face twisted into a scowl. "That ain't the way Donovan wants it. You'll talk before we're through. Okay, boys, let's get her outta here."

As the men advanced on her Denim tried to raise to her feet, but she was just too weak and shaky and she collapsed back onto the floor.

The door to her room opened. Then Denim heard it gently close. Slow footfalls crossed the floor. The room fell silent for several seconds before she heard a familiar voice.

"I think you boys have had enough fun for one night."

"We ain't even got started," one of the men said.

"Then you'd better get ready to die," the voice said smoothly.

Denim lifted her head to the source of the voice. Ben Straker, clad in a duster, was standing inside the room, opposite the cowboys, with two six-shooters drawn.

Henderson spoke up. "This ain't none of your affair, Straker. Donovan asked us to handle it. As far as you're concerned, it's finished."

Ben nodded. "You go back to Donovan and tell him it *is* finished."

Henderson squinted. "That ain't the way it's gonna be."

"Doesn't take much courage to rough up an unarmed girl. Any of you got the guts to draw on me?" Ben challenged.

"Think you can take all of us, Straker?" Henderson laughed.

Ben's lips peeled back in a chilling smile. "Try me."

The standoff lasted for many seconds. No one made a sound except for their breathing. Ben held his ground in complete confidence, his eyes never veering from Henderson, whose own boldness was starting to crack in the awareness that if shooting should start, he'd be the first to get it. The look on Ben Straker's face guaranteed that.

Finally Henderson broke the tense silence. His face

was glossy with sweat. “All right, Straker. I ain’t that keen on killin’ no woman anyhow. But it’s gotta be *you* that answers to Mr. Donovan.”

Ben nodded. “That’s fine. Now I’d like one of you fine gentlemen to go find old Tom Becker and have him get this lady’s horse ready. Have him bring it by the hotel. Around the back.”

The cowboys filed from the room with Ben’s guns trailing them until the last one had exited. Ben closed the door, hesitated, then turned to Denim. The girl’s face was damp with whiskey, her mouth stained with the blood she’d drawn from the cowboy’s hand, and her long hair tangled and disheveled. She was looking back at Ben, though her expression was vacant.

She had regained enough of her senses to realize that Ben Straker had saved her life. Yet it was impossible for her to feel any gratitude toward him. All she could feel was a cold hatred.

Ben holstered his guns and said: “You’re leaving Prosperity and don’t ever be riding back.”

Denim continued to regard him with an empty stare.

“Makes up for nothing, I reckon,” Ben said, a little sadly. “I understand your hating me. But it’s my profession. And I don’t make apologies for it.”

And then—in a swift movement Ben withdrew his short-barreled rifle from under his duster and took it firmly by both hands, raising it high over his head and slamming the stock down with a crushing impact on

Denim's outstretched hand. Her left hand. Her gun hand. Denim emitted a quick, agonizing scream before blacking out from the pain.

"I'm sorry, Laurie," Ben said. "But I have to make certain you won't be coming back."

Chapter Ten

The Finding

It was George Merrell's man Luther who found her. He'd gone out in the buckboard after breakfast to make some supply purchases from a friendly neighbor named Hank Ferguson when only a couple of miles from the farm he saw a horse standing by its lonesome just off the dirt trail into town. Curious, Luther climbed down off the rig and tentatively limped through the tall grass toward the animal, who did not appear fearful at his approach; in fact, seeming to invite the man to come to him with a faint whinny and jerking of his large head—though as Luther got nearer the horse started to react with a slight defensive behavior. Luther had a way with animals and moved slowly, speaking calming words until the horse once again appeared relaxed.

"What you doin' out here, fella?" Luther said . . . and

then he saw that the horse was *not* alone. What Luther presumed was its rider, a badly battered young girl, lay either dead or unconscious at its feet. Luther understood instantly that the horse had been protecting her. He quickly examined the girl, saw that she was breathing, and determined that she could be moved onto the buckboard. He explained his intention to the horse who followed close behind as Luther carefully lifted the girl and carried her the several yards to the rig.

He gently placed her in the flatbed and covered her limp form with some sackcloth. Before climbing back up onto his seat, Luther turned to the horse who was inspecting the rider laid out in back of the rig and said: "Reckon you'll be comin' with us."

George Merrell was doing some work around his property when he squinted through the bright morning sunlight to the sound of the approaching buckboard.

George was puzzled. It was about a three-hour roundtrip to Hank Ferguson's place. He didn't expect Luther to be back until early afternoon. He started out to meet the buckboard and the lone horse that trailed behind.

Once George got alongside Luther pulled in the reins. "Mistuh George," he said and he tilted his head toward the flatbed.

George walked over and glanced inside. His face instantly registered recognition.

"I know this girl," George said softly.

"Don't know what happened." Luther scratched the back of his neck and wore a concerned look. "Found her like this off the road on the way out to Mistuh Ferguson's. Looks like she might be hurt bad."

George nodded. "Yeh. We'll git her inside."

George hopped aboard and Luther rode the buckboard onto the property. Together they gingerly carried the girl inside the small ramshackle farmhouse and into George's room where they laid her on the bed.

"Want I should go fetch the doctor?" Luther asked.

The nearest doctor outside of Prosperity was in Barstow, which entailed almost a day's ride both ways.

George shook his head. "Don't know if that would do much good, Lucky," he said, his eyes never lifting from the girl. "Think it best if we just tend to her ourselves."

"I'll git some water," Luther offered and he hurriedly limped out of the room.

George stayed with the girl. He honestly didn't know if there was anything they could do for her. She looked in bad shape and he had no way of knowing whether she had suffered any internal injuries. But he was certain of two things: if she was busted up inside she'd never survive until the doctor arrived. And she did not sustain her injuries from falling off her horse. She had been beaten. He examined her crushed left hand. It was purple and swollen and looked as if every bone had been broken—and deliberately. George determined that if she pulled through she would never again have the use of that hand.

George and Luther tended to the girl through the day and into the night, keeping her cool with a moist cloth and periodically submerging her damaged hand into a pail of cool water to reduce the swelling. The girl still hadn't regained consciousness, but both her breathing and heartbeat were steady.

Finally George told Luther to get some rest; he would to sit up with her.

"You're tired too," Luther said. "I don't mind sittin' for a spell."

"No," George replied. "Might be needin' you to run an errand early tomorrow."

Luther spoke in a whisper. "You think she's gonna be all right, Mistuh George?"

George's voice was likewise low. "We've done all we can, Lucky. Dependin' on how she comes through the night, I might be sendin' you to fetch that doc."

"I hopes yuh does, Mistuh George," Luther said. "Truly hopes yuh does."

George agreed with a nod.

Sunlight filtered into the bedroom as dawn came to the valley. George had stayed awake all night, leaving the girl's side only to refill his coffee cup. He was relieved, if frankly surprised, to see that the girl was holding her own. The time was right, he thought, to send Luther on his errand. George quietly crept from the bedroom and walked across the house to where Luther slept. He gently tapped on the door, but when his friend failed to respond, he opened the door and peered inside. To his surprise, Luther wasn't there.

"Mistuh George," his friend's voice sounded behind him.

George turned around. Luther was grinning broadly at him.

"Got the horse all saddled and I reckon I'll be off."

George returned the smile.

"I just knowed she was gonna be all right," Luther said. "I knowed it."

It was shortly after noon that Denim began to stir. She became restless, as if she were having a bad dream. George was sitting at the supper table in the next room smoking a cigarette when he heard her moan. He got up and went over to her. The girl's face was drawn and her complexion pale. George wet the cloth from the water in the basin and gently patted her face and forehead. He didn't want to startle her awake.

Gradually, Denim's eyes began to open. They focused on George but she was still numb and disoriented and she regarded George emptily—with neither recognition nor apprehension.

George spoke gently. "Glad to see you're still with us."

Denim didn't reply. She let her eyes drift around the strange room.

"You're safe," George explained.

Denim's brow creased as her eyes once more landed on the cowboy.

"Don't expect you to be doin' much talkin'," George said.

Denim's lips parted slightly. "I can talk," she said weakly.

She grimaced and tried to raise her injured hand, which

George had carefully wrapped in a makeshift bandage while she was asleep—more so that she couldn't immediately notice the severe damage that had been done to it. George leaned over and gently placed her arm back down on the bed. Fortunately Denim didn't resist.

"Looks like you had an accident," George explained calmly.

Denim's expression tightened and she started to shake her head. Her gestures only confirmed for George what he had already suspected. But he didn't want to pursue the matter, and it was not yet the time for the girl, either.

George poured her a cup of water from the pitcher on the bedside table and placed it to the girl's lips. She took a few short sips. As he took away the cup the girl thanked George with a softening of her eyes.

"Anythin' else I can git you?" George asked her.

Denim weakly shook her head, but a second later her eyes widened. "Daybreaker," she said.

"Daybreaker?" George repeated with an inquiring look.

Denim frowned. "My horse?"

George gave a little smile. "He's out back. Fine animal. Followed you and my man all the way here. We'll take care of him 'til you're able."

"He's—gotta know I'm okay," Denim said.

"Your *horse*?" George questioned, lifting his eyebrows.

Denim nodded.

"Tell you what I'll do," George offered. "You just stay put and I'll bring him 'round to the window so he can take a look at you."

His suggestion brought a slight smile to the girl's pained expression.

George went outside to the fetch the horse. While at first tentative, Daybreaker soon seemed to realize that the man posed no threat and allowed him to lead him by the bridle to the side of the farmhouse. There George tapped on the glass to alert the girl and then prompted the animal to look inside the window. He admittedly felt a little foolish, but when he saw the excited reaction of the horse as he appeared to recognize the girl, tossing his large head jubilantly, he was both amused and heartened. George peered in through the windowpane to observe a genuinely happy expression on the girl's face. George was certainly not unfamiliar with animal intelligence, but he had never seen anything quite like this before.

George patted the animal's crest. "I think you're all the doctorin' that little girl's gonna need."

It was just after sundown when Luther rode back to the farm. George heard his approach and reckoned that he must have been riding with the wind. What concerned him, however, was that he heard only one set of hoofbeats ride onto the property. George got up from his chair and hastily went outside to meet him.

"Din't make it all the way, Mistuh George," Luther said breathlessly as he dismounted. "Met some folks on the road who told me that the old doc up and died just two days ago. No doctor in Barstow fer 'bout the next week. How's the little missy doin', Mistuh George?"

George creased his forehead. “It’s her hand I’m worryin’ ’bout.”

Luther shared his friend’s concerned expression. “Way I see it, you ain’t got no choice but to take her to the doc in Prosperity.”

George spoke a little impatiently. “Don’t you think that woulda been the first thing I’da done? But that sawbones is Donovan’s man, and unless I’m missin’ my guess it was somehow Donovan’s doin’ that put that girl in her condition.”

“Why yuh be sayin’ that, Mistuh George?” Luther asked.

George’s tone softened. “Just a feelin’ I got, Lucky. I seen that girl in town. And I know what happened to her was no accident with her horse.”

Luther nodded vigorously. “I know what you’re sayin—’bout that animal. He ain’t the kind to be buckin’ her, ’lessun he got spooked by a snake or somethin’.”

George dismissed that possibility. “If he was spooked, most likely he’da run off.”

Luther pondered for a moment. “You’re right, Mistuh George. And I seen him there standin’ beside her like he was watchin’ out for her.”

George said mellowly: “He was.”

Although Luther had been out on the road for the better part of the day, he offered to cook some bacon and biscuits for supper. George declined, explaining that he’d fried a couple of eggs earlier. After checking in on the girl and finding her fast asleep, he stepped outside onto the porch and rolled himself a cigarette, which he lit with a flick of a match against his boot heel. He knew it was important that he still get her looked at by a doctor—especially her damaged hand. He considered his options while he puffed on his cigarette and finally came to the realization that he had just the one. He would have to ride her into Prosperity himself and have the doctor there treat her. He didn't like the idea of exposing the girl to travel so soon, but he knew that the only way he'd coerce Dr. Brennan to come out to the farm would be at the point of a gun, and George wasn't looking for that kind of trouble. He decided that for the girl's own good he would plan the trip into Prosperity the next morning.

But he found himself contemplating what sort of trouble that would bring.

George knew that whatever had happened to the girl had occurred in Prosperity. Therefore he thought it best not to tell her where he would be taking her. She was still weak but now more alert, and he didn't want to upset her. If there was a problem he would handle it once they got to town. He made her comfortable in the flatbed of the buckboard, which he'd lined with sheets and blankets, and started on the road shortly after seven. Traveling this way—and riding slowly so not to jostle her too much along the often rough road—he reckoned they would arrive in Prosperity just around noontime.

The ride was slow and uneventful. The girl slept most of the way, which George thought was a good thing. The sky was blue and cloudless and as noon approached the sun was a large white ball distancing the eastern mountain ridge. George rode the buckboard through the trail that provided the most shade, courtesy of the sparse cottonwoods that bordered the road just north of the rich watering stream where George and Luther often liked to fish.

George never packed his gun when he rode into Prosperity. From his experiences there he knew that bringing along a side arm would only invite trouble. Men were always itching for a fight and, knowing of his former reputation as a gunslinger, would surely hope to provoke him into a fight where he might be forced to draw his gun and maybe—*maybe*—shoot him dead, thus earning Brock Donovan's favor. George maintained that he was never going to be the reason for any man to enter Donovan's good graces.

Of course, it was more likely to go the other way, which would also satisfy Donovan, using his influence to convict and hang George on a trumped-up murder charge.

The buckboard rumbled into town and George directed the horses down the main road to where an alley intersected. The town seemed quiet and only a few curious or disapproving stares met George as citizens recognized his familiar buckboard. He drew the rig deep inside the alley, away from curious eyes, next to the municipal building where the sheriff's office was housed, and halted the team. He glanced over his shoulder into the flat bed. The girl had been asleep, but once the buckboard stopped her eyes slowly opened. George hopped off the buckboard and stepped over to the girl.

"I'm gonna see if the doc is in," he told her calmly.

"Where—are we?" she asked faintly, fluttering her eyelids.

George ignored her question. "Just wait still," was all he said.

Dr. Julius Brennan's office was on the second floor of the barber shop, which could only be accessed by climbing a narrow stairway located in the alley. George climbed the rickety steps and entered the office. There was no one waiting to see the doc, and George wasn't even sure if Brennan was around. He gave the door a hard slam behind him, and a moment later Dr. Brennan scurried out from his examining room. He stopped dead in his tracks when he saw George Merrell.

"You're a man of medicine," George said in a pleasant enough tone. "I got someone with me who needs lookin' after."

The doctor was hesitant. Like everyone else in Prosperity, Julius Brennan had no wish to upset Brock Donovan by having any dealings with George Merrell—professional or otherwise.

"I'm rather busy today," he replied officiously.

Brennan was a small man, slight in stature and in build. George knew he would be an easy man to intimidate, but that wasn't his purpose, even though he could instantly detect the man's nervousness.

George glanced around the empty waiting room. "Yeh, and I got forty pigs that need tendin'."

Brennan coughed. "Well, you see—" he started to explain.

George abruptly cut him off. "I got a girl outside who's in pretty bad shape. You're the only doc within twenty miles of here, and she can't be waitin'."

"Well, I . . . ," Brennan stumbled.

"You took some kind of an oath, didn't you?" George said, growing impatient.

Brennan continued to stall.

George said more calmly: "Doc, this is strictly 'tween you an' me. And if it's the money you're worryin' 'bout, I'll pay your fee."

Brennan cleared his throat as his eyes nervously darted about the room. "Very well, then. Bring her in."

"That goes both ways, doc," George added. "What I say 'bout this bein' just between the two of us."

Brennan looked a bit relieved. "Yes, of course. 'Course."

George held his stance for a few more seconds, eyes locked on the doctor, then he went outside and down to the buckboard to get the girl. A few curious townspeople had followed the rig to where it had parked and were now standing across the street watching George. He ignored them and covered the girl in one of the blankets lest she be recognized, and carefully carried her up the steps to the office.

"Bring her into the examining room," Brennan said.

George did as instructed and gently laid the girl on the table, lifting both sides of the blanket away from her face and body. He glanced at the doctor to check his expression.

Brennan reacted, though George wasn't sure if it was due to recognition or her condition.

"Y'know this girl, doc?" George asked outright.

Brennan hesitated. "I'm—not sure," he replied, and he walked over to the basin to wash his hands.

"I'll be waitin' in the next room," George told him.

The examination took about twenty minutes. George tried to read the newspaper but found that he could not concentrate. After a bit he got up and began pacing the floor. Finally, impatient, he walked back into the examining room.

The girl lay still and quiet on the table with her right arm flung across her eyes. George could not tell whether or not she had been crying, but if she had George could guess the reason. Brennan had exposed her hand during his examination and the girl must have finally seen the full extent of the damage.

"She's going to be fine," Brennan said to George as he wiped his hands with a towel. He spoke with emphasis so that the girl could also hear his encouraging prognosis. "Some bruises, a mild concussion, but she'll be up and around in a few days."

George gestured with a flick of his eyes to the girl's gauze-bandaged hand, which was supported in a sling.

Brennan replied with a tilt of his head that he and George move out into the waiting room.

"Okay to be leavin' her alone?" George asked quietly.

Brennan nodded.

The two men stepped outside where Brennan spoke softly. "I can't do a thing for her hand," he said, adjusting his spectacles. "No one can. Maybe . . . right after it happened, with the right kind of surgery. It'll heal, but she'll never be able to use it to any great extent."

George merely blinked.

Brennan nodded. "I don't know if it's any consolation, but my first thought was that I might have to amputate. Fortunately, the damage is not as severe as it appears."

George's lips tightened. "But she'll still be a cripple?"

Brennan drew a breath. "She may regain some use of it—with therapy. But it will be limited."

"Doc, could she have got that from fallin' off a horse?" George questioned carefully.

Brennan looked puzzled and uneasy. "Is that what she said?"

"Didn't tell me nothin," George replied sharply. "I'm askin' *you*."

Brennan paused before he answered. "In my professional opinion—no. Not given the appearance of the injury."

George nodded and for a moment he appeared contemplative. "I'll be takin' her along with me, doc. What should I be doin' to care for her?"

"She's healing as well as can be expected. Might have some headaches and spasms for a few days, but those'll pass."

"I'm talkin' mostly 'bout her hand," George said.

"I gave her some powders for the pain. If necessary, you can refill at the druggist. The bandage will have to be changed every couple of days. I'll give you some extra gauze to take along with you. Beyond that . . . nature will have to take its course."

George nodded. He reached into his pocket for some money. "How much I owe you?"

"Three—" Brennan began. Then he paused and said: "Make it a dollar."

George lifted his eyes to the doctor. "That's mighty generous," he remarked as he handed Brennan some silver.

Brennan accepted the money and thrust it into his pocket. "Now I'll be asking you a favor," he said in as stern a voice as he could muster. "I'd appreciate it if you wouldn't be making any more visits here."

George gave the doctor an ironic smile. He didn't say a word, just went back into the examining room to get the girl.

He was surprised to see her on her feet. Though she still looked pale and a little unsteady, George immediately detected a steely determination in her character.

This was confirmed when the girl said firmly: "You mighta had to carry me in here, but I aim to be walkin' out on my own."

They left the office and George helped the girl down the stairs to the buckboard. A few people were milling about across the street. George paid them no mind but noticed that a few seemed to recognize the girl as they began talking amongst themselves with their eyes focused on her. Denim just regarded them with a cold stare and an icy silence. She knew she was back in Prosperity. And she wasn't about to be hiding from its citizens.

"I'll sit up front," she said to George.

"You might be more comfortable lyin' in the back. We got a pretty long ride ahead of us."

Denim looked suspicious. "To where?"

"Back to my place," George said casually. "That's where you'll be stayin' 'til you're back on your feet."

"Don't need no one lookin' after me," Denim responded in a slightly offended tone.

George drew a breath and made his point firmly. "I told the doc I'd be carin' for you. 'Sides, what am I s'posed to do with your horse?"

Denim's face brightened at the mention of Daybreaker. She seemed a bit embarrassed, but quickly resumed her posture. "I'll still be sittin' up front."

"Suit yourself," George replied, and he helped her up onto the seat.

George then went round the other side and climbed beside her. He clucked at the two-horse team and the buckboard rolled down the alley. George decided to take the back road out of town lest more curious onlookers congregate on the main street.

It was a quiet ride back to the farm. George did not initiate conversation, and he was a taciturn man in any case.

It was Denim who finally broke the silence. "Just so you should be knowin'," she said, "I wasn't cryin' back there in the doc's office." She waited for a response, but George didn't provide it. "It's just that the doc was playin' with my hand, twistin' it and all . . . and it hurt."

"I figgered as much," George replied.

"Still does."

"Reckon it will for a while."

"Why'd you bring me to Prosperity?" Denim finally asked a short while later.

"Wasn't no closer doctor," was all George said.

Denim cocked her head and took her first good look at George. "I thought I recognized you. You're that fella I saw in the saloon," she remarked.

George didn't acknowledge. He raised his head and squinted against the bright midday sun.

"S'pose I should be thankin' you," Denim said lowly.

"No need. It was my man who found you," George said.

Denim seemed a bit frustrated by George's reticence. "Well, don't you even wanta know my name?"

"If'n you feel you should be tellin' me."

"Reckon I should. After all that you done fer me. It's Laurie."

George nodded, his eyes fixed on the road ahead.

"You got a name?" Denim asked.

"George."

"George," she repeated with a nod.

Denim decided against further talk and settled back in her seat and tried to enjoy the ride. But after traveling for some distance she started to get sore and the pain in her hand began to flare up. She refused to admit this to George, but he could quickly recognize her discomfort by her grimaces and fidgeting. He pulled in on the reins and halted the buckboard under the shade of an old cottonwood.

He fixed his eyes squarely on her. "Somethin' tells me you're gonna be stubborn. I admire the fact you're tryin' to be brave, but don't be so mule-headed you won't be askin' for help if you need it."

Denim gazed down at her bandaged hand and it looked to George as if her defenses were about to crack.

"It—hurts somethin' awful," she admitted.

George gave a nod. "I know it does," he said sympathetically. He ventured: "And I'm guessin' you got another hurt that's painin' you just as much."

Denim gave him a surprised look but didn't acknowledge.

George said gently: "When you're ready we can talk 'bout it."

Denim lowered her head. "I knew another stranger that was good to me," she said sadly, in a distant voice. "Only he wasn't like he seemed." In an unconscious gesture she cupped her right hand around the bandaged left.

"When you're ready," George said again.

They rode back onto the small property encircling the farm. Luther was outside tending to the pigs when he saw them come down the road. He smiled with delight as he noticed the girl was sitting up next to George. He climbed over the fence enclosure and limped over to them.

"There's the man to be thankin'," George said to the girl, nudging his head forward toward Luther.

Denim took an immediate and particular notice of Luther's game leg. She saw how the pronounced limp sure didn't seem to be slowing his progress.

"Well, well, I'm pleased," Luther said as he greeted the buckboard. "I'm truly pleased."

George made the introductions. "Luther, this is Laurie. Laurie, Luther."

"Mistuh George calls me Lucky," Luther grinned, exposing a mouthful of white teeth. "Like it if'n you'd be callin' me that."

Denim couldn't help smiling at the man's warmth and genuine likability. "And you can call me Denim," she returned.

George's expression became alert. "Denim? As in Denim Ryder?"

Denim offered a slow nod of acknowledgment. And a lot became clear to George in that instant. Although he'd never seen her perform, he knew of Denim Ryder's reputation . . . as one of the West's most acclaimed *left-handed* sharpshooters.

"Lucky," George said to his man, "help Miss Ryder from the wagon."

"Gladly," Luther said as he offered a hand to the girl.

Denim accepted Luther's eager assistance.

"Hope you're hungry, Miss Denim," Luther announced. "Fixed yuh both a fine lunch: salt pork and sourdough biscuits. My specialty, Mistuh George says."

Denim nodded, not having the heart to tell this good man that the ride had made her nauseous and she doubted she could digest a morsel of food. But she let him escort her toward the house. First, though, she had to make a stop to see Daybreaker, who was housed inside the barn.

George didn't immediately follow. Instead he sat back on the buckboard and built a cigarette, striking a match against the side of the rig to light it. He watched as the smoke trail lazily drifted upward.

After a bit he rode the buckboard to its place at the side of the barn, unhitching the team and leading them inside to their stalls. Then he ambled into the house. Luther and Denim were hitting it off fine, though the girl finally had to admit that she had no appetite and just felt like resting for a while. Luther understood and helped the girl into the bedroom where he made up her bed. Of course, there was no woman's nightwear available and so Luther provided her with a pair of his own pajamas. He carefully helped her off with the sling and then left the room while she dressed herself, after which he went back inside and slipped the sling back on over her shoulder and arm. Once Denim was comfortably in bed. Luther came out to sit at the table with George. He was carrying Denim's clothing in a bunch.

"Gonna tend to the girl's clothes," Luther announced. "Looks like they haven't been cleaned for a spell."

George looked amused. "You're one fine nursemaid, Lucky."

"Took a fast likin' to that girl," Luther admitted. "She gonna be 'round for a while?"

George nodded thoughtfully.

"She tell yuh what happened?" Luther asked quietly.

George shook his head, again thoughtfully.

"Doc fixed her up, though," Luther said.

"Best he could," George replied, adding: "Not much he could do with her hand."

"That—that's a right shame," Luther said sadly.

George could only acknowledge with another slight nod.

Denim was exhausted after her trip into town and slept through the day. Toward nightfall the eastern skies began to darken and it looked as if rain were imminent. George had done some work around the farm most of the afternoon and was glad he'd completed his chores before the rain came. Taking note of the gathering clouds, he reckoned they might even be in for a big storm. They were overdue for one; the past weeks had been exceptionally dry. Luther made sure that the horses were settled inside their stalls and the pigs and whatever chickens he could round up placed in their own enclosures. He could tell by their unsettled behavior that they too anticipated some rough weather. When he came inside he saw that George was feeding wood into the potbellied stove. With the rain could come a colder night than usual.

The two men at last sat down to supper. Luther wondered aloud if he should waken the girl and ask if she was up to joining them. George considered for a moment and then suggested that they should just let her rest. They could put some food aside for her if she got hungry later.

After supper the two men sat quietly outside on the porch until the rain started. As George had predicted, it quickly turned into a downpour that brought them inside. Luther checked in on the girl, still fast asleep, and then retired for the night while George sat up with a cup of coffee.

Thunder rumbled, accompanied by fierce bolts of lightning that George observed through the window. Like the parched, arid earth, he was grateful for the rain and felt comfortable inside his little house, which was well protected against the weather.

It was after midnight that the storm subsided. George always appreciated the crisp freshness in the air after a heavy rain, and he stepped outdoors to savor it. The clouds were passing west, opening to reveal a deep blue sky glittering with countless stars. Off in the distance the mountains appeared as bold shadows against the expansive fabric of night. George sprinkled tobacco from his pouch onto some paper and rolled a cigarette, which he could enjoy while taking in this breathtaking vista, one of which he never tired. He'd sleep well tonight.

The door opened behind him. George turned, expecting to see Luther, but instead it was the girl. She was in the pajamas that Luther had provided, with a small blanket thrown around her shoulders.

"You shouldn't be out here, dressed like that," George said. "Gets cold after a rain."

Denim walked over beside him, tucking her right arm under the sling. "Just for a bit," she said, ingesting a deep, fortifying breath of the clean, fresh air.

"Storm wake you?" George asked.

"Mmm-hmm," Denim nodded. "Been awake I reckon for 'bout an hour. Tried to get back to sleep but I guess I'm plumb rested out."

"Care to sit?" George offered, indicating the two chairs off to the side of the porch.

Denim shook her head. "Not just yet."

For several minutes they stood in silence, enjoying the calm and the stillness of the night, which was only periodically disturbed by the chirruping of hidden nocturnal creatures scurrying forth from their dwellings following the rain. For Denim these surroundings were so much a reminder of being back on her grandpa's farm that she suddenly found herself trembling. George noticed and adjusted the blanket around her.

"You're cold," he said.

"Ain't just the cold," Denim admitted. "Maybe we *should* sit fer a spell."

George looked at her. "All right, but inside. There's hot coffee on the stove."

They went inside the house where George added more chopped wood to the fire. He slid the girl's chair away from the table and positioned it closer to the stove and its warmth. He then held up the pot of coffee, but Denim declined.

"Don't care for it," she responded with a look that suggested she'd just bit into a raw onion.

"Well, you hungry then?" George asked. "I can heat up your supper. Nothin' fancy. Just beans and some of those biscuits left over from lunch."

Denim hesitated and George said: "Y'gotta keep up your strength. You ain't et a thing all day."

Denim finally agreed. George took the tin plate and placed it on top of the stove to heat it. Then after a few minutes he set the plate before the girl and supplied her with a fork. Denim still seemed reluctant to touch her dinner and George assumed the reason. She evidently had favored her left hand in all her tasks—from firing a trick shot to simply eating a meal. Now even lifting a fork in her right hand was awkward for her.

"You'll get used to it," George said gently.

Denim managed a few bites before she put down her fork. Instead she reached for a biscuit that she ate out of her working hand.

"You and Lucky have been awful good to me," Denim said, a little shy at expressing her appreciation.

George was equally reserved at acknowledging it.

Her eyes lowered, the girl then said tentatively: "Was wonderin' if . . . you could be teachin' me how to use my other hand."

George seemed a little perplexed by her request. "Ain't no teachin' involved," he said. "You'll learn yourself just by doin'."

"That ain't what I'm askin'," Denim said with mild impatience. She hesitated, then clarified: "I want you to be teachin' me to use a gun."

George fell silent. He eased back in his chair with his coffee cup held in both hands, as if to warm them. Then he saw the girl look at his use of both hands with a sad expression. George caught on and subtly removed one of his hands from around the cup. His eyes leveled on the girl.

"Thinkin' of going back out with the shows?" he finally asked.

Denim did not answer.

George paused before he came out with his next question. He spoke to the point. "How 'bout gettin' even with whoever did this to you?"

For the first time Denim looked George directly in the eye. "There's more to it than that," she said in a muted voice.

George wasn't going to push the girl for her story. That would be her choice when and if she was ready. And when he could see that she was not yet of a mind to be telling, he rose from the table. "Whyn't you try to get some sleep."

"You still ain't answered my question," Denim said.

"No. And I reckon I won't 'til I get a few good hours of shut-eye."

Denim was unable to fall back asleep and she laid awake in her bed until she saw the first rays of sunshine filtering through the windowpanes. When she finally got up she noticed her jean wear neatly folded on a chair across the room, looking and smelling freshly laundered. With stubborn determination she made up her mind to dress herself all on her own. She carefully slid her arm out of the sling and went to work putting on her clothes. It was a slow, occasionally painful process, but she felt a sense of accomplishment once she was done.

She had decided to take Daybreaker out for a ride. It was a glorious morning, still fresh after last night's rain. Her horse needed the exercise and she wanted to prove to George and Lucky—and mostly to herself—that she could do things on her own. When she entered the barn to fetch her horse she was surprised to find Luther up at this early hour giving Daybreaker a brushing. He had on an old pair of bib overalls but no shirt covering his brown body.

"Mornin', Miss Denim," Luther greeted cheerily. He then exclaimed: "Why, Miss Denim, you is already dressed!"

Denim returned the greeting and walked over to her horse, which responded with instant recognition, nickering and rocking his head.

"Sure is a handsome animal, Miss Denim," Luther said. "And he does have a special likin' for you."

"Raised him since he was a foal," Denim said proudly. "Spoiled him too . . . and he knows it."

Luther snickered. "Surely does."

Denim began rubbing behind the horse's ear. "Been through a lot together," she said affectionately. "Reckon he's the best friend I got."

"Can never go wrong with a good animal," Luther remarked.

Denim became quiet, hesitant to ask him something that had been on her mind.

Finally: "Lucky, would it be wrong of me to be askin' what happened to your leg?" she said meekly.

Luther understood the reason for her question. "I don't

mind yuh askin', Miss Denim," he said, assuring her with a grin. "I ain't ashamed of it. Was born that way."

Denim paused. "Reckon you learned to live with it?"

"What choice have I got?" Luther shrugged, still maintaining his grin. "How yuh deal with the things life sometimes hands yuh is all due to yer thinkin'." He tapped a finger against his forehead for emphasis.

Denim nodded slowly and she looked thoughtful for a moment.

And then Luther's face took on a serious expression. "Miss Denim," he said quietly, "maybe it ain't my place, but if'n yuh wouldn't mind I'd kinda like to be sharin' somethin' with yuh."

Denim smiled her okay.

Luther put down the brush, patted Daybreaker's rump, and came round to the girl. He seated himself on a small stool and scratched behind his head.

He said: "Don't quite know where to begin . . . and if'n it'll even make sense to yuh . . . but my pa used to talk about what he called 'the wake of dawn.' Never could figger out what he was meanin' 'til one day I came right out and asked him 'bout it. As he told it, it was sort of a new beginnin' that a person can make for themself—if they choose to. That every man wakes to a new day."

Denim looked at him, her head cocked, her expression mildly perplexed.

Luther coughed deliberately. "Miss Denim, now don't yuh go getting' mad, 'cause I wasn't listenin' on purpose, but I—I heard some of what yuh was talkin' to Mistuh George 'bout last night."

"Oh?" Denim said, her eyes lowering as her body shifted. She leaned back against the stall slants.

Luther coughed again, and this time he spoke to the point. "What I'm sayin' is that no matter what happened to yuh back there, yuh got a chance to make a new start for yerself. And it's just plain wrong if'n you're thinkin' 'bout . . . well, what yuh might be thinkin'."

Denim stood very still, and then, without uttering a word, she walked over to Luther and hugged him with her right arm. Luther appreciated the embrace but wasn't sure if his words had made an impression on the girl.

She simply smiled at him. "Thinkin' I'd take Daybreaker for a little exercise."

"You up to it, Miss Denim?"

"You don't gotta be worryin' 'bout me and Daybreaker," Denim replied.

"No . . . s'pose I don't," Luther sighed. He gave his head a shake and walked over to the saddle. "Let me ready him for yuh."

Denim added emphatically: "We're as much a team as you and Mr. George."

Luther turned to the girl and grinned in agreement. "Yes'm."

Denim's morning ride through the valley was just what she needed—and Daybreaker too. He was eager for exercise and a few times attempted to break into a gallop. But Denim kept her horse at an easy pace, her good hand resting on the pommel. She returned to the farm feeling refreshed. The ride had cleared her head and given her time to think. She knew that both George and Luther were aware of her intentions. What they could not understand was why she remained determined in what she had to do. All her life she had harbored the most bitter hatred toward Brock Donovan. But she had felt something distinctly different towards Ben Straker. She wasn't sure if it was love exactly; that still seemed a foreign emotion to her. But she had cared deeply for him . . . and perhaps in her own way she had loved him. Yet now . . . she almost hated him worse than Donovan—and it went beyond him killing her grandpa. Because all the while he was courting her, making promises to her, he had known what he'd done. He wanted to come back with her to the farm where he knew her grandpa lay dead from a bullet from his own gun. He had lied to her. He had deceived her and betrayed both her trust and her affection.

She rode Daybreaker into the barn where Luther helped her dismount and then led the horse to his stall and began removing the riding gear. Luther was grinning, but he was quiet. Denim understood why. She wanted to say something to him, but she knew that whatever she said would not be the words he'd want to hear. She gave Daybreaker an affectionate nuzzle and then walked from the barn. She was absorbed in thought and even a bit in her own guilt, and failed to notice George standing in the shadows of the overhang on the porch sipping a cup of coffee. He watched her cross the yard toward the house with her long strides.

Her head was slightly lowered, Stetson tipped to protect her eyes from the glare of the sun, her gold-reflected hair streaming out behind her from under her wide-brimmed denim hat.

He admitted that he was becoming attracted to her.

George sighed as he ruminated on the realities of there being a romance between them. He had a few years on her, that was a fact, and he was not a man easily given to affection or understanding the complexities of a woman's needs. But what he was experiencing was a pure emotion, one not compromised by age or lack of insight into the female mind. He was simply captivated by her. She was a lovely girl, sweet, maybe a bit naive- and as much as it also concerned him, he admired her spunk. She was someone George could feel a closeness toward, just as he felt a yearning to care for her.

George was a quiet man who mostly kept his thoughts and his moods to himself. That aspect of his character would make it difficult for him to express what he was feeling to the girl—if he dared to do so. He'd probably end up making a damn fool of himself. But maybe . . . in the off chance that she felt something similar toward him, that would be reason enough for her to stay her course.

As Denim started up the steps of the porch she lifted her head and finally saw George. They exchanged a pleasant smile.

George simply said to her: "Feel like givin' that hand some practice tomorrow?"

The girl's smile instantly broadened into a wide grin.

Chapter Eleven

The Saloon

A tinny cowboy tune issued from the player piano, punctuating the Saturday evening gaiety in the Golden Circle Saloon as its patrons enjoyed individual amusements ranging from drinking and teasing the serving girls to engaging in a serious game of faro at the table in the back room. Joe McDonald was busy filling drink orders with the same miserable look on his face, even though he was assured of a good night's business.

Off in a lone corner sat two men and the tension that surrounded them was heavy.

Brock Donovan's anger was so intense that his breath was short and each sentence he spoke was punctuated with heavy wheezing. He was seated at the table that was reserved for his periodic visits to the saloon, sitting across from Ben Straker. He was venting his fury at the gunman, and felt more secure about doing so in a place filled with his own people.

"You crossed me twice, Straker," Donovan growled through his spit. "You walked out of our arrangement . . . then you interfered with my men."

Ben sat calmly, discarding Donovan's rage.

"The way I saw it, there was no need to kill that girl," he explained in a slow voice.

Donovan's eyes widened with almost a crazed look. "Easy for you, Straker, you ain't the one she come gunnin' for."

Ben took a sip of his whiskey. "You won't have to worry about her gunning for you, Mr. Donovan. I took care of that."

"Purty sure of yourself, huh?" Donovan said, red-faced.

Ben offered a deliberately sunny smile. "Am this time."

Donovan breathed deeply. "Well, just so you should be knowin', your little spitfire came into town yesterday. Yeh, her and a farmer named Merrell. They paid a visit to the doc's."

"Not much you don't know about what goes on in this town," Ben commented.

"Damn right," Donovan grumbled in agreement. "I make it my business to know 'bout *everything* that happens here."

Ben said: "There's nothing any doctor can do for her."

Donovan's expression became curious.

Ben spoke confidently. "Go talk to him. Ask him about the girl's hand."

"What about her hand?" Donovan demanded.

"She shoots with her left hand. That was her skill . . . which she doesn't have anymore."

Donovan was thoughtful for a moment. "Maybe it ain't the girl I'm so concerned with now."

Now Ben looked interested.

"That—farmer she's with," Donovan went on. "Merrell. George Merrell. Used to be one of the best guns in the Southwest."

Ben considered. "You don't say."

"He's a peaceable man now," Donovan said in a contemptuous tone. "Went agin me and chose to become a poor soil worker. But I don't know how peaceable he's gonna be if'n that girl gets to talkin'."

"Well . . . you let me worry about the farmer." Ben lifted his whiskey glass in a salute.

Donovan's eyes glinted. "And the girl . . ."

Ben just tilted his head back and closed his eyes.

Chapter Twelve

The Romance

They'd hiked into a field not far from George Merrell's small acreage where George set up ten empty cans he'd brought along in a sack as targets on the length of a fallen tree. He kept the distance short, about ten yards, and stepped back to where Denim was standing.

"You any good with a gun?" Denim asked teasingly.

"Had some practice," George replied nonchalantly. He was wearing an old checkered shirt opened several buttons below the collar with the sleeves rolled up to his elbow. His tanned chest and arms were already glistening with sweat from the hot afternoon sun.

Denim was quietly skeptical. George was the rugged type, but to Denim he just didn't look the kind to be handy with firearms.

He said: "Reckon I should take a few practice shots . . .'case I'm rusty."

He had strapped on his gun belt with six-shooter fitted into its single holster. He practiced a few hand-to-hip maneuvers, though his awkward procedure and dudelike stance confirmed Denim's doubts about his ability. She rolled her eyes.

"Guess I'm ready," George said.

And suddenly his pose shifted. His hand swept with lightning speed toward the holster, withdrawing the revolver and twirling it in a swift single movement. He fanned the hammer with a quick action, discharging all six bullets, each hitting its mark and flinging each of the cans into the air in a somersault motion. He then twirled the revolver and fancy-maneuvered it back into his holster.

Denim's eyes bugged. "George Merrell, you was joshin' me. Why, you're almost as good . . ." Her voice trailed off.

George eyed her sideways and smirked. "Almost."

"I can't figger you, George Merrell," Denim said with a perplexed expression. "You can handle a gun like that yet you never carry no side arms."

"That's why," George replied modestly. "Learnin' to shoot a gun's just a skill. Don't take no bravery. If a man's a coward, a gun won't make him no stronger."

He emptied the shell casings from the chamber, reloaded, and handed the gun to Denim. She accepted it in her right hand and almost immediately she could tell it didn't feel proper. She hefted it and tried some simple maneuvers but the gun was heavy and felt uncomfortable in her grip.

"Don't worry 'bout bein' fancy yet," George advised. "That'll come with time."

"Just seems strange," Denim said sadly. "Been handlin' a gun all my life and now I can't even hold it right." She tried to justify: "Maybe it's the balance."

Wordlessly, George stepped over behind the girl, gently taking her arm by the elbow and raising it level with the perched cans, then smoothly sliding his calloused fingers toward her small, soft hand and aiming the barrel of the revolver at the four remaining targets. Much to George's relief Denim did not resist his closeness or his touching her.

"Got your aim?" George asked.

"Mmm-hmm," the girl said in a purr.

George slowly drew his hand away. The girl fired once—and missed.

"Drat!" she exclaimed. "Overshot by a mile."

She took her time steadying her next shot . . . and tried again. Another miss. Gradually she emptied the chambers and only one of her shots just winged one of the cans.

"This is gonna take a lot of practice," she sighed heavily as she dropped the revolver to her side.

"Won't happen overnight," George remarked. "Why don't we have some of that picnic lunch Lucky fixed for us?" he then suggested.

Denim handed him back the gun. "S'pose so," she said petulantly.

George pointed to a leafy Freemont cottonwood. "We can eat under the shade of that tree."

George spread out their lunch on a blanket and they sat down to eat. It was just past midday and the grass was bone-dry despite the heavy rain of the night before. Luther had packed some canned meat and canned fruit and, of course, some sourdough biscuits. George built a small fire and brewed a pot of coffee while Denim drank water from a canteen.

After a while Denim asked: "Say, where'd you learn to shoot like that?"

"Just somethin' I picked up," George said dismissively.

Denim eyed him suspiciously. "No, sir, no one can just 'pick up' shootin' like that."

George just smiled and ate a bit of ham. "Reckon not."

Denim looked sourly at her bandaged hand.

"Still hurtin'?" George asked.

"Off and on," Denim replied casually. "But havin' this bandage is a plain nuisance." She sighed. "Don't know if I'm too anxious to see what's under it, though."

There was nothing George could say to soften that concern. Instead, he sighed deeply and let his eyes soak in the tranquility of their surroundings. The sky was high and blue. A welcome motion of air produced a slight cooling breeze and whistled through the foliage of the old cottonwood.

"You can't help but feelin' peaceful when you're out among nature," he said contentedly.

"That's how I used to feel when I was back home with my grandpa," Denim said softly, a hint of pain in her voice.

"Where d'you call home?" George asked.

"A little ranch called Caillou."

"Your grandpa still live there?"

The pain in Denim's voice was now visible on her face. She struggled with her words. "No. He—he don't."

"Dead?" George asked bluntly.

Denim gave a quick nod.

George offered a slight, sympathetic expression. "Sorry to hear that. What 'bout your folks?"

"You want me to be tellin' you?" Denim snapped.

George backed off. "Don't want you to tell me nothin' you ain't got a mind to."

Denim slowly got to her feet and took a few steps away from George. Her back was facing him when she said: "S'pose I should. Reckon you already figgered out part of it."

George remained quiet and let Denim make the decision for herself.

Denim sat herself back on the grass, though near to George. She looked closely at him, deeply into his eyes, searching for the sincerity and, most importantly, the honesty she hoped to find there. George's gaze met hers and he never flinched. Denim sighed . . . and she told him the story. Although it was difficult, she felt instantly trusting of George and comfortable enough not to hold back any of the painful details. George listened, patiently, never interrupting, his expression firm, only his eyes occasionally flickering with emotion. Emotion that was especially raised when she mentioned the name Brock Donovan.

When she was finally finished all George said was: "You've gone through an awful lot for such a young girl."

Denim wore a rueful smile. "Sometimes I don't feel so young."

"I 'preciate your tellin' me," George said in a low voice, and he rose from the grass. He placed his hands firmly on his hips and gazed out far into the distance. "Girl," he then said after a lengthy pause, "if'n I was you I expect I'd be feelin' the same way. But I ain't you, and all I can see from where I'm standin' is a bitter mean hatred that could destroy everythin' that's special 'bout you. Killin' Donovan ain't gonna bring your folks back. Lettin' him live is a far worse punishment. He's full of a poison that he has to live with every day. As for that Ben Straker—well, fellas like him only end up one way. He'll get his 'reward' sure enough—but blood for blood ain't gonna fix what you got inside you."

"For most of my life it's all I lived for," Denim said reflectively. "To see Donovan pay for what he done."

"Gave you the wrong kinda purpose," George returned. "The memories you have of your grandpa . . . what you see around you here and now—that's what you should be rememberin'. You had bad things happen in your life, Laurie, no mistakin' that. But now you gotta make good things happen. All this hate your carryin' will sure enough stop you from ever knowin' happiness."

Denim furrowed her brow. "Someone else told me that," she said, thinking of Marie DuBois.

"And you want it straight?" George added. "Your hand

ain't no use to you anymore. Not as a gun hand. You'd never stand a chance goin' up agin Donovan and his lot. All you'd be doin' is givin' him the satisfaction of another killin'." He said definitely: "I don't wanta see that happen."

George steadied himself for what he was about to say next. "You could have a life, Laurie. A good life. Stayin' with me and Lucky on the farm."

Denim regarded George with a bewildered look.

"I think you know how we both care for you," George went on. "How I care for you."

Denim was silent; she cast her eyes down to the grass. Her features were soft and delicate. She looked like the innocent girl George knew she really was . . . if she could be purged of the hatred she'd burdened herself with for so many years. But George could also recognize the danger that walked alongside her beauty and spirit. It marked her like a brand. Yet whatever her decision, it would be *her* choice. No one could decide it for her since she was clearly of her own will. She could either ride out her years consumed with a festering need for vengeance or she could choose the path that George had taken. It was a decision that he had never regretted making.

George stretched out his hand and Denim received it, though somewhat tentatively. He raised her to her feet and their eyes met. His were strong and firm; the girl's soft and moist, as clear and blue as the vast skies that surrounded them. He started to wipe a tear from her eye with his thumb but, embarrassed, she turned her head away. George gently turned her face back toward him.

"You don't got to be ashamed, Laurie—not with me," he said.

The girl managed a smile and said: "I know you're a good man, George Merrell."

George brushed back the hair from her face. "Then put aside your hate . . . and give yourself a chance at a better life."

Denim was hesitant. "I—just don't know."

"What makes you unsure, Laurie?" George asked with concern. "Is it bein' with me . . . or that can't you let go?"

Denin carefully considered her answer. "Once I thought I knew what real carin' was," she admitted, gazing up at George with a sadness in her eyes.

"Trust me, Laurie. You never have to have no fears," George assured her.

"I been through an awful lot of hurtin'," Denim sighed.

"I know you have," George said compassionately.

"And maybe . . . I ain't smart to be trustin' agin so soon."

"I ain't never gonna be askin' you to feel somethin' that you ain't got inside of you, but that's a question you have to answer yourself," George said. "Is that how you really feel, Laurie? Deep inside . . .'bout me?"

"No," Denim said softly, thoughtfully.

"Maybe I won't ever give you the life you're deservin' of," George told her. "But I'd work hard to make you happy."

As if she were responding to an impulse beyond herself, Denim lifted herself on her toes and tenderly kissed George on his bristled cheek. He responded by wrapping his arms around her waist and drawing her close.

While the girl did not voice it, in her thoughts she was thinking how much George Merrell reminded her of her grandpa. His strong, silent ways and what seemed his genuine goodness. She never could have thought that she could permit herself to feel the same way about a man after surrendering herself to Ben Straker and then discovering the truth. But now . . . being with George, she felt different. She believed that she could set herself free and listen to her heart, with no doubts or apprehensions . . . and her heart whispered to her that perhaps she could give herself to George and be with him.

Denim moved away from George and stepped out from the shade of the cottonwood. She took a long, absorbing look into the valley. This was clean land, not claimed by Donovan, nor stained with the blood of his many evil deeds and betrayals. The wide blue skies opening upon grasslands stretching as far as the eye could see. The tall green grass sweeping gently and rhythmically in the faint afternoon breeze. She captured these few moments in her memory, understanding that if she was ever to truly find peace, it could be here. And if she could every really find happiness, maybe . . . it could be with George.

Later they strolled back to the farm. Luther was outside scattering seed to the chickens. He watched them approach and saw that they were holding hands. He also noticed the first hint of happiness he'd seen on the girl's face. Luther wiped his hands on the apron tied around his waist and walked over to greet them.

"That was a fine picnic," Denim said to him, smiling

her dimpled smile. George just walked by and threw his friend a wink.

"Hot damn!" Luther exclaimed, sweeping off his straw hat and slapping it against his thigh.

In the days that followed a transformation occurred in Denim Ryder. She regained her health and began to adopt more of a feminine attitude. She spent hours riding with George in the valley and insisted on helping with chores around the house—as much as she was able to manage with her handicap. George continued to take her out for shooting practice, to the point where she was starting to hit her targets. But it was understood that these lessons were intended more for therapy than to eventually exact a revenge against the two men for whom Denim still felt a cold hatred. Once she became more proficient at firing a gun from her right hand she confessed that she would imagine the faces of Brock Donovan and Ben Straker pasted on the targets, thus making her aim more steady and sure.

But with George and Luther's constant caring, the girl inevitably mellowed. It surprised even herself that she could finally start to feel content with her life. She could finally embrace the happiness that she had denied herself.

Finally the day came when it was time to have the bandage from her hand permanently removed. Luther carefully cut the gauze while George sat next to her, holding her other hand. It took Denim a while to finally muster the courage to look, and what she saw distressed her. Her hand was bent and twisted and scooped like a claw. She knew at once that she would never regain complete use of it. She sat quietly for several moments and then she called upon her reserve of strength and merely sighed. Her pained expression gave way to a look of embarrassment.

"You gonna be all right, Miss Denim?" Luther asked.

Denim nodded.

Luther said: "How it looks don't make no difference to us. Ain't that right, Mistuh George?"

"No difference at all," George agreed solemnly but sincerely.

Denim smiled appreciatively and, without uttering a word, reached for one of her tight-fitting gloves and fitted it over the twisted fingers of her hand. It was silently understood that the glove would now become a permanent fixture.

Later that day when she and George went for a walk to the stable, Denim said in a far-off voice: "I know why he done it."

George looked at her, not comprehending.

"Why he done what he did to my hand," Denim said.

George let her go on.

"He didn't want me to go after Donovan," the girl explained. "He stopped me the only way he could."

George asked: "You up to tellin' me 'bout Straker?"

Denim squinted. "I already told you 'bout him."

George nodded. "Most, I reckon," he said. He paused before adding: " 'Ceptin' your feelin's toward him."

Denim stopped dead in her tracks. "Why d'you gotta be knowin' that?" she said in an offended tone.

George took a breath. "Because if you choose to share my life, I think it best if there ain't no secrets."

Denim lowered her eyes. "It ain't no secret," she sighed. "I—thought I cared for him . . . and him for me. Maybe . . . even with what he knew he done he *did* care."

"Cared enough to—" George said moderately, his eyes lowering toward her gloved hand.

Denim raised her head and looked directly at him without acknowledging his remark.

"It's behind you now, Laurie." George said, pulling her slight body close to his. "Has to be."

Denim spoke with firmness. "Reckon the one thing you gotta be knowin' is that if he hadn't busted my hand . . . and if I hadn't met you an' Lucky, and you both bein' so good to me, I'd still be aimin' to kill 'em."

"I know," George said softly.

Denim drew a long breath. "So you don't gotta go thinkin' I still got feelin's for him, George Merrell."

"Only for me?" George ventured.

Denim closed her eyes and answered him with a kiss against his cheek.

Chapter Thirteen

The Courage

The following day George decided to make a trip into Prosperity. He was up early, while Denim was still asleep, and told Luther that he was going into town to pick up some coffee and groceries—and a special present for the girl. Through his livestocking he had managed to put aside a bit of money that he had never had a need for spending. Without elaborating, George confided in his friend that he had a surprise planned for that evening. Luther nodded his head knowingly and offered to prepare a special meal for supper—maybe even a berry pie.

George wanted to make the trip fast so he decided to forego the buckboard and instead tossed a couple of saddlebags over his horse. He entertained the thought of maybe stopping by the saloon for a quick drink once he was done with his shopping. He knew almost certainly that presented the potential for trouble but he was feeling mighty good and in the mood to celebrate what he was proposing to do that evening.

The town was generally quiet in the morning. Unless escorted, no women ventured into the town during the week and most of the men were busy at work inside their various establishments. The only people most likely to be seen wandering the streets were the cowboys, but they usually never rode in until later in the afternoon.

George hitched his horse to the railing post outside of the general store and ambled inside, taking his time in choosing just what foodstuffs to purchase. The store owner, a carefully groomed gray-haired man named Grayson, initially eyed George with suspicion, but said or did nothing to antagonize him once he saw that George was clearly of a mind to spend a few dollars in his establishment. After George was done he packed his purchases into the saddlebags and then went back inside to select a present for Denim. By this time the owner's wife had come out and George asked for her advice for a nice ladies' gift. When she asked him what exactly he had in mind George shifted from one leg to the other and replied somewhat uneasily: "Somethin' suitable for an engagement present."

Grayson overheard and said with surprise: "You gettin' married, Merrell?"

"Ain't sure," George replied with a shrug.

"Not sure?" Mrs. Grayson questioned.

"Reckon I'll find out tonight."

Mrs. Grayson smiled but her husband went about his

duties with a concerned look stamped on his face. The store didn't have much in the way of female trinkets and George finally settled on the best it had to offer: a gold-plated locket. He laid down seven dollars for the piece and another dollar fifty for a chain. Mrs. Grayson offered to gift-wrap the purchases and George gratefully accepted.

He felt good as he left the store, even though he didn't know how Denim would take to the gift—or how she would respond to what he was planning to ask her. That presented him with some apprehension . . . and another reason why the thought of a cold glass of beer appealed to him.

The saloon opened for business at eleven, and it was just past the hour that George went inside. He figured a quick beer and then he'd head back to the farm.

He saw Marie DuBois sitting at one of the tables, a bottle of gin and a glass before her.

George heaved a breath. He expected to be asked to join her and he wasn't keen on obliging. But he immediately noticed how the woman didn't look well. Her face was haggard and there was a sickly pallor to her complexion. Of course, she wasn't plastered in makeup at this early hour, but she still looked terrible.

Joe MacDonald saw George approach the bar and just grunted. The miserable look etched into his unpleasant features made it clear that neither George's presence nor his patronage was appreciated.

Marie just regarded George dully—almost as if she didn't recognize him.

"Just gimme a beer, Joe," George said to the burly bartender.

Joe poured him a glass on tap.

George looked over his shoulder at Marie. *What the hell,* he thought. *Might as well be social.*

He paid for his beer and walked over to her table and sat down.

Marie looked at him silently, her expression drawn, her eyes glazed.

"You look terrible, Marie," George observed.

"And good morning to you," Marie replied, deadpan.

"Hungover?" George asked. "Or just gettin' started?"

Marie frowned. "I'm dying, George," he said. "You know it and I know it."

George took a swallow from his beer. He wiped the foam from his mouth with the back of his hand.

"You been dyin' for years," he said without sympathy. He leaned back in his chair. "You know, Marie, I can't figger you. You say you come out here for your health, yet ever since I knowed you all you do is work on killin' yourself faster."

"Not fast enough," Marie stated.

George pushed his worn Stetson back over his forehead and wiped his brow. "Now there's some self-pityin' for you."

It was not yet noon and he could tell she was well on her way to a good drunk.

Marie had been drinking a lot. Ever since she took it

upon herself to reveal to Denim what she had learned about Ben Straker. And how Denim so refused to believe her that it caused a rift in their relationship. And then the girl had suddenly disappeared, and Marie couldn't find out what had happened to her. If she was alive . . . or dead. No one would talk to her. Brock Donovan had shut the door on her and even people in town had begun to shun her. Marie had become so consumed by guilt and uncertainty over the girl's fate that she decided to lose herself in the only friend she felt she had left—her gin bottle.

"I'm all used up," she said, focusing on George. "I'm no good to anyone anymore. Not even myself."

George said simply: "Marie, I'm feelin' just too good to wanta go there with you agin."

"What have you got to be feeling so good about?" Marie asked glumly.

George eyed the woman carefully. Denim had told him about the friendship they'd had when she first came into town. But George also knew about the other "friendship" Marie enjoyed with Brock Donovan. He decided against saying anything.

At that moment three of Brock Donovan's ranch hands burst through the batwings into the saloon. They didn't recognize George since his back was facing them. But one of them was Ned Randolph, who had a particular enmity for George. The other two were Nick Lawson and Steve Bronson.

The cowboys all lined up at the bar.

"Get us some whiskey and a coupla bottles to take with us, Joe," Ned Randolph demanded loudly.

Joe obliged. "You boys celebratin'?" he asked gruffly.

"Donovan's in a might generous mood," Ned explained. "Gave us the day off."

"And we know how to put it to good use," Steve Bronson added mischievously, punctuating his remark by hitting a bull's-eye into the barside spittoon.

"Yeh, and the others'll be ridin' in later. You'll see a good business today, that's for sure," Nick Lawson piped in.

Joe could smell the liquor already wafting off their breath. He said sternly: "Just tellin' you boys that if you're plannin' on lettin' off steam you'd be smart to do it elsewhere."

"Right now all we want is a little relaxin'," Ned assured him. "The fun comes later. Right boys?"

Marie was listening to their talk. "If they see you sitting here, their fun starts now," she said quietly to George. "The loudmouth is Ned Randolph."

"Ain't lookin' for trouble," George said calmly.

Marie smirked. "You never do. But it seems to find you all the same."

"Howdy, Marie," Ned Randolph said from the bar, grinning through his yellow teeth.

Marie replied with a curt nod. She had no use for most of Donovan's ranch hands and had a particular dislike for Ned. He was a bully and a brute.

With his back to the bar, George couldn't see Ned squint

and level his attention suspiciously on the table. But Marie could—and she flicked her eyes to her companion. George seemed oblivious, even when he heard the heavy thumping of boots start toward the table.

"You can't leave well enough alone, could you, Merrell?" Ned's antagonistic voice spoke from behind George.

Joe McDonald cleared his throat mightily from the bar as a warning to Ned not to start anything.

George ignored Ned's words and the hot, humid breath on the nape of his neck, but Marie's expression grew tense.

Ned was scornful. "Yeh, it's all 'round town how you brought that girl back into town after we run her out."

Marie's interest was instantly aroused. Her heavy-lidded eyes suddenly widened and shifted from Ned to George.

"George, is Denim all right?" she asked in a suddenly sober voice.

"She's fine, Marie," George answered straightly.

"Sure she is," Ned said. "The pig farmer here brought her into town and had the doc patch her up."

"George . . . what happened to her?" Marie asked desperately.

George kept his face forward. "She's all right," he said again.

"Maybe talkin' to the back of your head is better'n lookin' at your face, Merrell, but I don't like it," Ned growled, and he forcefully kicked at the back legs of George's chair, swinging him partway around.

George instinctively shot up from his seat and faced Ned.

"That's enough!" Joe bellowed.

"Shut up, Joe!" Ned exclaimed, his expression contorted with rage. "You work for Donovan like the rest of us. So if you wanta be interferin' in this . . . you'll be answerin' to him." He stepped close to George and spoke into his face. "You keen on that girl, pig farmer? 'Cause if'n you are, maybe once I tell you what I done to her you'll wanta do somethin' 'bout it."

"He's just trying to provoke you, George," Marie cautioned.

"You shut up too, Marie," Ned shouted sharply. "This don't concern you, so don't go makin' it none of your business."

George stared steely-eyed at Ned. "I know full well what you done to her, Ned."

"Then make your move," Ned grinned balefully.

"George, don't be a fool!" Marie pleaded.

George stood firm. He said with disgust: "Don't worry, Marie. I wouldn't dirty my hands fightin' someone gutless enough to beat up on a girl."

Ned was seething. "Callin' me a coward? You better back up those words, Merrell."

George noticed that Ned's left hand was firm on his hip, about an inch from the handle of the Colt resting in his holster.

Joe McDonald started to come around the bar, gripping his double-barreled "peacekeeper." Ned's two companions quickly jumped the barkeep, each grabbing an arm and seizing the shotgun.

"Just you and me, pig man," Ned hissed—and then he slapped George hard across the face with the back of his hand. George flinched but maintained his posture.

"You're still yella, that's why you're never heeled," Ned spat. "But I aim to be finishin' this." He tugged off his gun belt and threw it to the floor in front of George, who didn't so much as look at it. Still grinning through bared teeth, Ned strode over to Nick Lawson and pulled out the revolver from his holster.

"Pick it up," Ned demanded, gesturing loosely with the revolver to the holstered gun on the floor.

George didn't budge.

"If'n you don't, I swear I'll kill you on the spot," Ned vowed.

"He's not bluffing, George," Marie said nervously, realizing that George was backed into a corner with only the one chance to get out.

"Damn right I ain't bluffin'," Ned said.

Finally George knelt to a crouch, eyes still tight on Ned, and withdrew the gun from its holster. He held it low at his side. By now Ned had a murderous glint in his eye. He wanted to see George Merrell dead.

"We'll do this outside," Ned said. "Just that we have witnesses to say I gave you a fair chance. Get movin'."

"So you can shoot me in the back?" George said.

Ned shook his head slowly. "That wouldn't be fair," he said deviously.

George gave Marie a look of calm confidence and started walking, but slowly. Ned was behind him, keeping at a distance, but rapidly closing the space between them as George's steps slowed even more. Finally, impatient, Ned got near enough to nudge George with the barrel of his gun.

While walking, George had secretly twisted the gun in his hand, palming the barrel . . . and then once Ned jabbed him he swung around and smashed the walnut handle of his revolver into Ned's jaw. It made a sharp cracking sound as it connected, and Ned dropped to the floor. Before his still-armed companion, Steve Bronson, could make a draw for his weapon George had flipped the revolver into trigger position and aimed it at both cowboys. They carefully raised their hands and Joe snatched back his peacekeeper, likewise keeping it trained on the two. With the situation under control, George tossed his revolver aside. Ned was still conscious and made a pathetic reach for his Colt. George kicked the gun across the floor where Marie scrambled to retrieve it.

"Thanks," George said to her with a smile.

Marie just blew out her breath and collapsed back into her chair at the table.

"Still ain't over, Merrell," Ned said as he spat out some blood.

"You got off lucky this time," George said to him. "I owe you for what you did to that girl. But I won't hit a man when he's down."

"Don't let that stop you," Ned erupted, suddenly struggling to pull himself to his feet. He got about halfway up when George grabbed him firmly by the collar, yanking him upright.

"Since you're plain set on bein' stubborn, reckon there ain't no need for restraint," he said, and he drew back his fist and slammed it into the side of Ned's face, hitting him with such force that the cowboy flew across the room and tumbled over a back table. He lay sprawled on the floor, and this time he didn't get up.

Marie came over to George. She spoke quickly: "You'd better get out of town before the others ride in."

George nodded. Then he hesitated before he gave Marie an appreciative peck on the cheek.

He turned to Joe, still covering the two cowboys with his shotgun. "I owe you," he said appreciatively.

"Just don't come back, will you, Merrell," Joe returned.

Much later Ned Randolph and his companions sat on their horses just off the road outside of town. Ned had a cloth pressed against his mouth and was taking periodic and painful gulps from a passed-around whiskey bottle.

"You boys up to payin' a call tonight?" he said, his words slurred from the liquor and his injured jaw.

"Whaddaya got in mind, Ned?" Nick Lawson asked eagerly.

"Just aim to be finishin' what I started," Ned replied with a sinister inflection.

Chapter Fourteen

The Raid

When George got back to the farm he unloaded the foodstuffs from the saddlebags and handed them to Luther without mentioning his experience in town. Besides, he all but forgot about it once he saw Denim come running toward him as he walked his horse to the barn, where the girl had been grooming Daybreaker. She seemed especially happy today. He instantly shared her joy.

She surprised George when she threw her arms around his waist and hugged him tightly.

"Well, a man can't never say he's had a bad day when he gets a greetin' like this," George remarked with pleasure.

"You had a bad day?" Denim asked, her head cocked in concern.

George smiled. "Nope," he lied smoothly. And he kissed her forehead.

"Been helpin' Lucky with preparin' tonight's supper," Denim said proudly. She cast a furtive glance down to her gloved hand. "Done what I could."

"And I'm lookin' forward to eatin' it," George said with a wink.

Denim seemed a little embarrassed. "With such a fancy supper we're havin' I feel I should be dressin' in somethin' more fittin'. All you ever seen me in is jeans."

"Well . . . you look jus' fine to me," George said with a wink. He then squinted his eyes conspiratorially. "But I'll tell you. I been thinkin' that maybe we should take a run into Barstow this weekend and see if we can't fix you with some fancy duds."

"I never really ain't wore no dress before," Denim confessed. "Never had a mind to." She scrunched up her face. "Funny how I'm startin' to think that maybe I'd like to."

"Ain't so funny," George said tenderly.

Denim's blue eyes twinkled and she gave him a sly smile. "Reckon not."

She affectionately rubbed her cheek against his raised forearm. Her skin was soft and his muscle solid. She sighed.

And George was suddenly so filled with emotion that he knew he couldn't put off what he had to say to her. But he didn't want to do it here in the barn. He casually suggested that they take their mounts for a ride in the valley. Denim readily agreed.

They rode out to the little shaded stream where George and Luther liked to fish. There they dismounted and walked toward the edge of the water and stood under the high, leafy branches of an oak tree. George put his arms around the girl's waist and she hugged him back.

"Happy?" he asked her.

Denim gave her head a sturdy nod. "Reckon I am."

George cleared his throat. "Laurie," he said, focusing his gaze on the calmly flowing waters, "I ain't a man who always best knows how to express himself. 'Specially when it comes to . . . what I'm 'bout to say."

Denim looked up at George. Her sweet, open expression encouraged him to continue.

George roughly scratched the back of his head. "Well . . . outside of Lucky, I've lived most of my life alone. Then you came along and you fit right in—like family."

"You and Lucky made me feel like family," Denim returned in a murmur.

George drew in his breath. "Well . . . I—I was just wonderin' how you'd feel 'bout . . . well, maybe makin' it permanent."

Denim's lips parted in a gentle smile. Her clear blue eyes were lively. "What're you askin', George?"

George reached into his pocket and pulled out his little gift-wrapped package. "Would you be acceptin' this?" he asked.

"A present?" Denim said, surprised.

"Hope it's a mite more'n that," George replied.

Denim took the small package and for moments just held it in her hand, admiring it.

"It's real purty," she observed.

"Well, why don't you take a gander at what's inside," George suggested.

Denim sat down on the grass and laid the package beside her. George offered to help her unwrap it, but Denim gave her head a determined shake. This she had to do by herself. She opened the package slowly and carefully so as not to tear the decorative paper. George noticed with pleasure how after she got the box unwrapped she folded and tucked the paper inside the pocket of her jeans. When she removed the lid of the box she just gazed silently at the locket and chain inside. Gradually a big smile crossed her lips.

She carefully took out the delicate jewelry and dangled it in front of her eyes.

"Here, let me put it on for you," George said. Denim took off her Stetson and pulled up her hair in a bunch while George gingerly placed the locket around her neck. She clasped it with her hand and held it tight against her chest.

"Ain't never owned no piece of jewelry," she said.

George paused. Then he cleared his throat and said: "Now I'd like to be clarifyin' what I was sayin' before."

"Yes," Denim said firmly.

"Huh?"

"Yes, George, I'll marry you," Denim said instantly.

George looked dumbfounded. "How did you—" he started to say.

"I only knew a man like you just once in my life,"

Denim explained thoughtfully. "And I loved him like no other man . . .'til now."

"You sure, Laurie?" George asked cautiously. "You sure this is what you really want?"

Denim started to rise and George took her by the hand that she willingly offered and helped her up. In that moment, as their eyes met, he knew he didn't have to have any doubts as the love she clearly felt for him was perfectly captured in her features. Her eyes were dreamy and the smile that slightly parted her lips was pure and sincere. George cupped her face in his hands and drew her mouth toward his. If he'd never truly known the emotion of love before, he knew it now. At that moment. With her.

Denim drew back excitedly. "And I'd like for us to get married right here—where you proposed. Right under this here old oak tree."

"Suits me," George said agreeably. "Ain't much for churches. Always felt a lot closer to God outdoors in nature."

"Then I reckon I'm as happy as I'll ever be," Denim said briskly.

That night the mood in the small farmhouse was one of celebration. But during their meal Denim spontaneously initiated more serious conversation.

"Here I'm gonna be marryin' you and I don't hardly know much 'bout you," she said.

George spoke solemnly. "Don't care to talk 'bout my

past. Done some things, I reckon like a lot of people, that I ain't proud of."

Denim chewed her food thoughtfully. "The way I seen you handle a gun I figgered you can't have been a farmer all your life."

George smiled and said: "Was born on a farm."

"Here?"

"Missouri."

"But you left there?" Denim queried.

George nodded. "Was young. Went lookin' for adventure."

"And you found it?"

George nodded again. "Enough to make me realize that I wanted no more of it. So—I came back to farmin'."

"For a while Mistuh George led quite a life," Luther offered quietly.

George cast him a mild look of disapproval. "Someday I'll tell you more," he said to Denim. "But this night is for celebratin' what's ahead, not talkin' 'bout things that was done in the past." He gave a friendly smile. "Start talkin' 'bout that and you might change your mind 'bout marryin' me."

Denim returned the smile. "I ain't 'bout to be doin' that," she said with a twinkle in her eye.

After supper, Luther pulled out the fiddle he only rarely played and enthusiastically bowed songs that both George and Denim danced to for hours. Finally George asked Luther to play "Red River Valley," which was his favorite song, and he and Denim danced along to its slow rhythm, gazing at each other in the muted light of the table lamp, their eyes sharing their adoration and affection.

The night air was calm and still and the strains of the music drifted out into the valley. Not far from the house a spark of flame was struck and placed against the end of a fat cigar. The faint glow of the burning match briefly illuminated the mean-eyed, cruel face of Ned Randolph. He was sitting on his horse alongside his two companions, Nick Lawson and Steve Bronson. All were drunk—and the two cowboys restless.

"Sounds like they're havin' a good time in there," Nick Lawson observed. "Too bad we wasn't invited."

"We got our own invitation," Ned said.

"So what're we waitin' for?" Lawson said impatiently.

"The right time," Ned drawled, sucking on his cigar.

For the first time since Denim had come into his life, George laid in bed with her. It had happened so naturally, without words being spoken or perhaps even a sharing of conscious thought. As if some ethereal force had guided them to be together. Denim seemed content just being in his arms. She snuggled up close to his chest and listened to his heartbeat and the rhythm of his steady breathing. She loved the feel of his lean, strong body next to hers and absorbed the smell of his maleness.

"I feel so warm bein' here with you," Denim whispered. "Never knew it could be like this."

George lay in silence, gently stroking the long blond hair that cascaded alongside her face and over her shoulders.

Through the dark of the room just penetrated by a shaft of moonlight, George heard Denim sigh. Then her voice, softly: "George?"

"Hmm?"

"D'you think they gave my grandpa a decent buryin'?"

George was taken aback by her question and didn't answer.

"He was a good man," Denim said. "He deserved that at least."

"I'm sure he was taken proper care of, Laurie," George replied. His voice sounded strong and certain.

"Reckon I'd like to know for sure."

"We can always ride out there. If'n that's what you want," George said.

Denim was quiet for a moment. Then she said: "I'd like to."

For a long while Denim's thoughts stayed focused on her grandpa and she felt the emotion welling inside her. But she also felt safe and protected being close to George and knowing that he would always be there for her. And soon, her thoughts relaxed and she drifted off to a deep, comfortable sleep. . . .

It was after midnight when both Denim and George were wakened from their slumber. A whooping noise from outside had revived them. And just seconds later Luther burst into their room exclaiming: "The barn's afire!"

Denim was still half-asleep, but George was instantly awake and scrambled out of bed. He threw on his trousers and rushed outside with Luther. The barn was engulfed in flames. George knew it was useless to try and put out the fire and halted Luther from going to the well for water. It was futile. Any effort, no matter how determined, would not save the barn. The building was filled with dry hay and the wood materials used in its construction were old. The fire was already raging out of control. George's concern was for the horses trapped inside the conflagration, which he likewise felt had little hope of being rescued.

Moments later a panicked Denim followed the men outside and viewed the blaze. She could hear the horses neighing in terror from inside. She began screaming:

"Daybreaker! My horse!"

She started to run for the barn. George rushed after her and held her back. She struggled against his grasp but he held onto her tightly.

Luther saw her fear and suddenly half ran, half limped toward the barn. George called after him to stop, but Luther was unhearing. He flung open the big door then stepped aside as a gout of flame immediately lashed out. Once it subsided, he disappeared into the heavy smoke billowing from the barn.

Denim continued to scream, her sobs choking her and her eyes filling with tears. George hugged her. He felt helpless. He wanted to go in after Luther but knew that if he did the girl would surely follow.

"There ain't nothin' we can do, Laurie," George said through clenched teeth.

Denim was unreasonable, still attempting to fight her way out of his arms. "I can't let my horse die! Lemme go!" she pleaded.

"Fool girl. You go in there an' *you'll* die," George told her.

Moments later a horse suddenly burst forth from the barn. The animal was frightened and agitated, neighing and rearing its big body upward.

"Daybreaker!" Denim shouted as she recognized it was *her* horse that had escaped. Her whole body trembled with relief and she tried to break free of George to go to him.

"Let him calm down first," George told her.

And then the form of Luther reappeared. His head was bent and he was coughing from inhaling the smoke. Once a safe distance away he dropped to his knees. George and Denim rushed over to him.

"C-couldn't get no others, Mistuh George," he said through his coughing. "I tried . . . but just couldn't get no others."

"But . . . you—saved my horse," Denim stammered gratefully.

Luther looked up at her and managed a weak grin. "Yes'm."

Denim dropped to her knees and threw her arms around Luther, hugging him tightly. He was exhausted and short of breath and merely patted her on the shoulder.

"Weren't no accident," Luther said as he slowly recovered. "I seen lots of broken glass in there. Like from an oil lamp."

George bit down on his lower lip. "Deliberate," he muttered aloud.

"That's how I sees it. Mistuh George. Surely weren't no accident," Luther agreed, hefting himself to his feet. Both George and Denim took an arm and assisted him. The three stood and watched as the barn collapsed in flames. The frantic neighing of the three horses trapped inside had ceased. Daybreaker gradually calmed and Denim went over to comfort him.

Fortunately the night air was completely still. There was no wind blowing and the barn stood alone on a wide patch of soil, so there was little concern of the fire spreading and causing further damage to the property. But it would have to extinguish on its own. . . .

And by morning all that remained were the smoldering remnants of a fire. The little that was left standing resembled a charred skeleton. George and Luther slowly stepped through the rubble and the ash, littered with still-glowing embers. They found the bodies of the horses amidst the debris, their corpses badly burned with wisps of smoke still rising from the seared flesh. George's lips tightened. He quickly wiped his eyes with the back of his glove. Luther wondered for an instant if his friend was weeping at the senseless and cruel loss. But George was not that type of man. The disturbing and pathetic sight surely affected him, but George protected his emotions and would not reveal whatever it was that he was feeling. Luther accepted that his eyes were red-rimmed and irritated simply because of the smoke.

"Lucky," George said quietly. "I want you to ride out to Hank Ferguson's and see if you can't borrow one of his horses. Don't be tellin' him what happened . . .'less he asks."

"Yuh want me to take Miss Denim's horse?" Luther asked.

George nodded.

"Think he'll be fit for ridin'?"

"Reckon you'll find out."

Luther regarded his friend suspiciously. "What yuh got in mind, Mistuh George?"

George just stared at Luther for a long time. Finally he said: "Aim to be ridin' out to see Brock Donovan."

Luther's eyes widened. "You think that he—"

George simply replied: "Just don't be tellin' the girl."

Luther understood.

Denim had been up all night tending to Daybreaker. George and Luther walked over to her. The horse still seemed a little spooked as he snorted and backed up as the two men approached. Denim quickly relaxed him. Luther began petting the animal's flank and Daybreaker soon turned his big head toward him in calm recognition.

George said to Denim: "You think Daybreaker would be up to lettin' Lucky take him for a little ride?"

Denim looked tired and her expression was still strained from what had happened.

"After what Lucky done for him it's all right with me. If'n it's okay with Daybreaker," Denim said.

"Won't be takin' him far," Luther assured her. "And I sure won't be ridin' him hard."

"Whaddaya say, boy?" Denim asked her horse gently.

Daybreaker seemed to answer with a rock of his head and a nicker. George noticed that the horse's ears were in neutral position. He heard and he understood.

George affectionately patted the horse's rump. "Okay, Lucky, saddle up."

Shortly after noon a rider approached the little farm. George and Denim were inside the house when they heard the sound of hoofbeats nearing the house. George's expression was curious.

"Might be Lucky," he said, though he doubted his man would be back so soon and it sounded like a single set of hoofbeats outside.

George took the last sip of his coffee then got up from the table and walked toward the window. Much to his surprise, he saw Marie DuBois dismounting. He turned and looked back at Denim.

"Friendly company?" the girl asked.

"Reckon we'll see," George answered neutrally.

George opened the door and an anxious-looking Marie rushed inside. Denim smiled brightly when she first saw her friend, though her expression swiftly turned into concern when she noticed how Marie was out of breath and struggling to stifle a cough.

"You'd better sit," George told her.

Marie took a chair at the table and allowed a few moments to regain herself. Denim poured her a glass of cool well water from the pitcher, which Marie consumed gratefully.

"I just heard this morning," Marie said. "Donovan's boys are in town and they're talking about what they did."

George's jaws clenched so that the muscles in his cheeks stood out. He hadn't wanted the girl to know what he suspected and what Marie had just revealed.

Denim's expression tightened. "They—started the fire?"

Marie nodded briskly. "It was them. Donovan's bunch."

"*They* killed them horses . . . and coulda killed Daybreaker?"

George noticed the intensity start to grow in Denim. It concerned him and he spoke up to settle her. "I'm goin' out to see Donovan, Laurie. That's why I sent Luther to git me a horse. I wanta have a talk with him."

"Donovan's riding into town, I heard," Marie said. "He's probably there already."

Denim pulled away from the table and stood up, her expression suddenly fierce.

"I'm gonna to handle this," George said to the girl, firmly.

Denim swung around to face him. "You won't be handlin' nothin'," she said with ire. "That man's a liar and he won't be admittin' to nothin' he did."

"Prob'ly won't," George agreed.

"So what good's your talkin' to him?" Denim demanded.

George drew a breath, which he held in his chest. "'Cause I ain't even sure if it's Donovan himself who's behind this."

Denim regarded George incredulously. How could he dare to suggest that Brock Donovan might be innocent? She started to speak in protest but George cut her off.

George explained. "I'm serious, Laurie. Had a run-in with some of Donovan's men yesterday. Didn't wanta say anything, but Marie'll tell you."

Denim shifted her eyes to Marie and the woman gave an unhurried nod.

George said: "I reckon those boys got fueled up with liquor and decided to make up for . . . well, what I done to one of 'em."

"Ned Randolph," Marie offered. "He's a mean cuss. Just the type to do what happened here."

"Donovan knows he can't play me for no fool," George added placatingly as he poured himself another cup of coffee. "I'm the one man in the valley he can't try that with. I'll get the truth outta him." He glanced over the rim of his cup at Marie.

But Denim wasn't listening. All she could think about was that her beloved horse had nearly perished in a fire that Donovan surely had some part in. George could talk to the man all he wanted, but nothing would be settled. The man was as cold and lethal as a rattlesnake—and just as slippery. And Donovan would try it again . . . except maybe next time Daybreaker—or any of them—might not be so lucky.

The hatred she felt for Brock Donovan had again been ignited and was stamped on her face. Her features now registered an uncompromising determination. There was no longer any question in her mind that the man had to die. It was no longer just retribution for what he had done to her parents and grandpa. She had to carry through with what she'd intended or, she reasoned, none of them would be safe.

Her eyes veered to George's gun belt hanging on the wall. She hesitated just a moment before she casually stepped over to it, while George and Marie resumed talking with their attention on each other. Denim stepped before the gun belt and as unobtrusively as she could slid her good hand into the holster and withdrew the Colt revolver. She carefully tucked the gun into the waistband of her jeans and moved aside.

"I'm goin' outside to cool off," she then announced, grabbing her Stetson off the wall peg.

She walked briskly to the door, her hand pressed against her hip to shield the gun. All of a sudden George was overcome with an uneasy feeling and without saying a word to Marie rose from his chair. His fears were realized when he opened the door after Denim and saw the girl atop Marie's horse.

"Laurie!" he called out, but the girl had already snapped the horse into a run.

"George, you've gotta stop her," Marie said urgently once she followed him out onto the porch. "There's at least a dozen men with Donovan."

George looked strained. It appeared as if more lines had at once embedded themselves into his craggy features. The girl he loved was riding off to almost certain death, and for the moment there was nothing he could do.

He exhaled painfully. "Got no way of gettin' to town 'til Lucky get back."

"Well, when will that be?" Marie asked anxiously.

George paused, his eyes leveled on the dirt road, now whipped up in a cloud of dust from Denim's rapidly departing horse.

"In time, I hope."

Denim rode the trail into town as fast as she could—single-minded in her purpose and unmindful of the consequences to her own well-being. She had a score to settle and not even the devil himself could stop her now.

A short distance along Denim spotted Luther riding in the opposite direction, coming toward her. He was riding Daybreaker, holding what looked like a rope fastened to the bridle of a blue roan gelding trailing behind.

Luther recognized the girl and brought Daybreaker to a halt. Demin pulled her mount alongside.

"I'll be tradin' with you, Lucky," Denim said. "Need my horse."

Luther seemed uncertain. "But, Miss Denim—where . . . where yuh be headed?"

Denim quickly dismounted and walked over to untie the roan. "George'll explain," she said.

"No, Miss Denim," Luther weakly protested. "If'n your goin' to where—"

Denim looked at him solidly. "Just gimme my horse," she said.

Luther obliged, if reluctantly. He noticed the revolver tucked into the waistband of her jeans. "Please, Miss Denim . . . ," he pleaded.

Denim climbed atop Daybreaker. She managed a faint smile for Luther and then urged her horse into a gallop.

Luther was suddenly sweating. Wasting no time he lifted himself onto the other horse and broke it into a dead run, back to the farm, leaving Hank Ferguson's blue roan alone on the trail.

George and Marie were waiting when Luther whipped his horse up to the farmhouse. George had on his single-holstered gun belt fitted with a Colt revolver and was holding a .44-40 Winchester repeating rifle.

"We'll have to ride together, Mistuh George," Luther said in a rushed voice. "Hadda leave the other horse on the trail."

"You don't have to come, Lucky," George told him.

Luther was offended. "Just cause I don't walk right don't mean I can't handle a rifle."

George smiled appreciatively. He handed him the revolver. "Let's ride," he said, and he hopped up behind Luther.

Before they rode off George said confidently to Marie "Don't worry, Marie. We'll bring her back."

Chapter Fifteen

The Showdown

Demin took the back road into town. She didn't want to announce her presence prematurely. She figured that Donovan was probably at the saloon and so hitched Daybreaker to a post at the edge of town where it was unlikely she would be spotted, and went on foot around through the alley across the street from where the building was situated. She stood there, tucked into the shadows provided by the narrow opening between the undertaking parlor ("Jasper Morton, Proprietor & Owner: Fine Funerals at Reasonable Prices") and the town bank, and she readied herself for her showdown with Brock Donovan. She had a good view of the entrance to the saloon.

She held the Colt revolver in her right hand, limbering her fingers around its walnut grip to grow comfortable with its feel. She felt confident that even with her handicap she could outdraw Donovan, but had to consider that he would not be alone. She'd call for a fair fight, but wasn't sure how honoring his companions might be. She reminded herself that she was justified in challenging Donovan; the man had a lot to answer for. He could have let well enough alone . . . but he chose not to.

She wasn't afraid. She had been preparing her whole life for what was finally going to reach its end in the next few minutes. But as she stood alone with her thoughts, it seemed to her as if her recent past—the happy, peaceful time she had shared with George—had almost never happened. Strangely, those days now seemed to exist only as a memory—a brief and blurry respite from the purpose she could never completely abandon. To possibly be forever leaving that life . . . and especially George, saddened her, but she also realized that what she was set to do was her life's mission. It was what had consumed her every day for as far back as she could remember. Even with the promise of a better life with a man she truly loved, she could not turn her back on what she again acknowledged was her destiny.

She had returned to the identity of Denim Ryder.

Denim drew a deep breath, slid the gun into the waistband of her jeans, and started her walk across the street to the Golden Circle Saloon. As she moved her courage and determination traveled with her as her strides became stronger. She would stand up to the murderous Brock Donovan with all the fortitude that life had instilled in her.

A few of the town's male passersby stopped and looked curiously at the blue jean-bedecked girl as she stepped onto the boardwalk and approached the batwings of the saloon. Denim paid them no mind. Her attention was focused on the sounds of boisterous male cameraderie emanating from inside the saloon. She was certain that above the din she could recognize Brock Donovan's booming laugh.

A pulse now pounded at the side of her head. The realization hit her hard that within the next few minutes either she or Donovan would be dead.

But she allowed no time for doubt or hesitation. She swung open the batwings and strode inside. . . .

In a stroke of luck Luther and George came upon the blue roan gelding still on the trail. Luther slowed his horse's pace so as not to startle the animal, then George quietly hopped off and carefully approached the roan. At first the horse was tentative, backing off, but George was gentle and soon the roan was calm and steady enough for him to mount. George started off slow before breaking the roan into a gallop, then quickly picked up the pace. He rode holding the reins with one hand, his Winchester held upright in his other since the saddle had no scabbard. Luther's horse maintained a close distance behind. They raised dust with their pounding speed, but still had a couple of miles to go before they reached Prosperity . . . and every second counted.

Joe McDonald was tending bar and was the first to notice her. He loudly cleared his throat to call attention to her presence.

All eyes turned to the girl and a dark silence promptly descended on the saloon. Some of the men had been drinking and boasting, others were playing cards. What they all had in common was that they were the guests of Brock Donovan.

They were a dirty, unshaven, and mean-eyed bunch. Donovan stood out among them if only for his freshly scrubbed appearance and gentlemanly attire. He wore a laundered and neatly pressed gray coat with a starched white shirt and torquoise horseshoe-clipped bolo tie fastened under his collar. The man of respectability, Denim noted with a sneer. Among the sea of hostile faces he wore the most amiable expression. Outside of a quick flicker of surprise that crossed his features when he saw the girl standing in the doorway of the saloon, he appeared cool and composed.

Confident in his protection, he greeted the girl condescendingly. "Come on in, little girl, and I'll buy you a root beer." He emitted his overpowering laugh and his men dutifully joined in.

"Didn't come to drink with you, Mr. Donovan," Denim said with utter seriousness. "I'm here to make good on my promise."

Donovan's thick, wide face was jovial. "That's right," he said. "You said you was gonna . . . what was that, kill me?"

Denim slowly rocked her head. "Fairly, Mr. Donovan."

"And you was aimin' to shoot me for . . . ?" Donovan asked, gesturing broadly with his meaty hands.

Denim stood silently, her blue eyes fastening him with an icy stare.

"Three murders," she said flatly.

Donovan still didn't appear intimidated. At the very least he maintained his facade in front of his men. He looked around at them and joked: "Damn, she's got more guts than any three of you." Then he said to Denim: "If'n you was a man I'd put you on my payroll."

"Wouldn't expect you to remember, Mr. Donovan," Denim said, dismissing his bravado. "You done a lot more bad things since then."

"Reckon I have, little girl. But then—ain't we all." Donovan guffawed and again cast a sweeping glance at his bunch, who shared in his laughter.

Denim abruptly silenced all of them—but especially Donovan—when she slowly and with emphasis began reciting: "Cal Ryder . . . Amy Ryder . . . Jason Cole."

Upon hearing each of these names—names tied to the past he'd wanted buried and forgotten—a gray pallor seemed to consume Donovan and his fat, full face suddenly looked to deflate, becoming drawn and sunken.

But it was the mention of *her* name that had the most impact on him.

Amy Ryder.

Denim said: "Cal Ryder was my pa. Amy Ryder was his wife, my ma."

Donovan's reaction confirmed for Denim all she needed to know. As memories carted out by these names were evoked his emotion was genuine. Probably the first honest thing he'd ever expressed in his life. Donovan couldn't lie his way out of what he'd done. And Denim knew that, as well.

"I'm givin' you just one minute to clean yer conscience, if you can, Mr. Donovan," Denim said. "Then I'm callin' you out."

But Donovan surprised her. Suddenly there wasn't the aggression she had been expecting. Instead, the man seemed strangely subdued. His expression became thoughtful as he looked searchingly at the girl. He got up from the table. Two of the men sitting with him also started to rise, but Donovan waved them back down.

"How old are you, girl?" he asked with uncommon interest.

Denim cocked her head, curiously. "Twenty-two. If'n that matters."

Donovan walked nearer to the girl. He nodded slowly. "Yeh. That'd be 'bout right."

Denim remained puzzled, if firm in her words. "What're you talkin' 'bout?"

Donovan's eyes had lost their harshness. He spoke as if outside of himself. "She wrote me just once, reckon she hadda, and said that the baby died 'fore it was even born."

The hush continued among the others in the saloon. Even the serving girls were silent. They looked strangely at Donovan, puzzled by his rambling and unexpected shift in attitude, thinking that maybe he'd lost his senses.

"And all the time Cal Ryder was raisin' it as his own," Donovan continued.

Denim shook her head impatiently. "Don't be lookin' to stall this."

"It was the start of Elizabeth's sickness," Donovan said pensively. "She couldn't accept that I wanted to be with another. That I coulda fathered another woman's child."

Donovan hesitated before returning to the moment. His eyes locked on the girl's, penetrating her with their melancholy gaze.

"And that child was *you*," he said.

And with this admission Donovan studied the girl closely. He could never have noticed it before when they had first met, but now he was struck by the resemblance between the girl named Laurie and the still-vivid memory of the woman he had known over twenty years ago.

"You're lyin'," Denim erupted suddenly, her body trembling, the anger heavy in her words. "Cal Ryder was my pa."

Donovan spoke with resentment. "Cal Ryder wasn't no man. He could never father a child. He was weak. Dandified. Your ma was carryin' you 'fore she ever met the man."

Denim's working hand instinctively went toward the Colt tucked in the waistband of her jeans.

"You're a dirty liar'!" Denim spat indignantly. "You're makin' this up just so's I won't be killin' you."

There was a strange honesty in Donovan's eyes. "I ain't lyin, girl. But maybe I wish to God I was." He added with emotion: "I loved Amy."

"Loved her so much you had her killed," Denim stated accusingly.

Donovan's expression went blank. He looked at the girl for what seemed a long while before he simply replied: "Yes."

"That's all I ever wanted to hear you say," Denim said with satisfaction.

Donovan lowered his head slightly and spoke passively. "I killed her . . .'cause I couldn't let no one else have her."

The powerful Brock Donovan looked like a man defeated. As if the snake had shed his skin, revealing a vulnerable underbelly. Denim observed his sorry figure but could not find it in her heart to feel pity for Donovan—even if what he was saying was true: that he was her birth father, which she could not bring herself ever to accept. Too many years of hatred toward him would not allow for such an emotion. Nor could there be forgiveness. In truth, she simply felt numb. She never fired her long-intended bullet into Donovan, yet the man seemed as destroyed as if she had. The satisfaction she had felt at his confession disappeared.

She remembered what George had said: that it was a far greater punishment to let a man like Brock Donovan live on with his sins. She now understood what he meant.

Denim noted that several of Donovan's men were now regarding him with expressions suggesting disgust. The formidable Brock Donovan, the man whom many of them feared and held in respect, looked about as helpless as a baby. They were simple but hard-edged cowboys, uncomplicated, with a basic way of looking at things, with no understanding of sentiment—and the way they saw it, Donovan had been brought to his knees by a mere girl.

Ned Randolph was among that group. He'd been doing a lot of drinking and suddenly felt contempt for the man who had been his boss.

"You talk 'bout us havin' no guts," he said to Donovan. "She's callin' you out. Stand up to her."

Ned knew that Donovan was full of talk. Now he dared him to prove his mettle—even if his opponent was just a young spitfire. He was bored and craved some action.

Donovan turned to Ned, who was already on his feet. "Lessun she wants to take aim, no one is drawin' his gun," he ordered.

Some of the men started to laugh. Ned was bolstered by their encouragement. He edged away from the table where he and his companions had been playing five-card draw.

"Remember me, little girl?" he said to Denim.

Denim took a quick study of the man. She had only a hazy recollection of his face. But she could not place when or where she had seen it.

"You took a bite outta my hand," Ned reminded, thrusting his hand out with the scar still visible. "The night Donovan ordered us into town to take care of you."

Denim's eyes quickly flashed in recognition, like a

spark ignited into a flame. Her expression grew taut with repressed rage.

"Shut up, Ned," Donovan barked at the man.

"And that ain't all," Ned went on, doing his damndest to provoke her. "Who d'you think started that little fire at the pig farmer's? And who d'you think gave us the order to do *that*?"

Denim's face went even harder as her blood quickened. Her eyes shifted from the taunting Ned back to Donovan.

"Don't be listenin' to him," Donovan said, his eyebrows arched.

"You ain't his daughter anymore'n you're mine," Ned snorted.

"Don't be oversteppin' your bounds, Ned," Donovan said brusquely. "You're forgettin' who runs this town."

"Thought I did," Ned replied with a sneer. "Also thought you was a man with a backbone."

Denim shifted her weight to her other foot and said to Donovan: "I don't believe a word of what you're sayin' . . . but I knowed what you done, and I don't intend to see you do no more harm."

Ned looked pleased. "There you go, Donovan. She made the call."

Donovan looked behind him at Ned, then back to the girl.

"No," he said firmly.

"Donovan, you're skunk yella," Ned yelled. And fueled by alcohol and his volatile rage he impulsively drew his revolver and twisted it toward Denim.

Ned Randolph was drunk, having consumed many shots of whiskey throughout the day. But Donovan was slow. He stepped in front of the girl to protect her, but didn't have time to defend himself by reaching for the derringer he secreted inside his coat pocket before Ned plugged him with a single shot. As Donovan groaned and dropped heavily to his knees, his hands clutching at his belly wound, Ned whooped.

Donovan fell over onto his side, breathed heavily for a few moments, and died.

Ned Randolph's move was so sudden and unexpected that Denim stood momentarily paralyzed, unable to make a grab for her weapon before Ned had his Colt trained on her. Two of the cowboys quickly rushed Denim, disarming her. She started to struggle, but was no match for the strength of the men who took her by both arms and held her securely.

"Donovan took your bullet, girl," Ned hissed at Denim, "but we're still finishin' what we started." He'd tasted blood and was clearly thirsty for more.

Joe McDonald had been standing silently behind the bar. He lowered his hands behind the counter and started to reach for his peacekeeper.

Seven more men quickly took up sides with Ned. Watching them leap up from their tables to join him, Joe knew he'd never have a chance and slowly brought his hands up to the bar without anyone noticing.

One of the cowboys got up to protest. Ned swung around and aimed his .45 Colt at him. The man quietly sat down.

"Either you boys are with me, or sit quiet," he said. He cast a menacing glare at the saloon girls who had scattered about the room after the shooting. "And that goes for you all as well."

One of the men holding Denim asked deviously: "What're you plannin', Ned?"

Ned looked at the girl through eyes narrowed into slits. "Justice," he replied boldly. He walked over, took Denim's clean Colt, and holstered it. The weapon that he had fired, he dropped to the floor. "She killed Donovan and's gotta pay. Take her outside and we'll string her up."

His party whooped their approval.

Ned turned to the seated cowboys. "You all saw what happened. Everyone in town knows she was gunnin' for Donovan." He looked especially hard at the bartender. "You knowed it too, Joe."

Joe said nothing. The situation was out of control and these men were too dangerous to deal with.

Ned Randolph and his bunch formed a circle around Denim and hustled her through the batwings. The sheriff, Tom Brough, was already out on the street, walking toward the saloon to investigate the gunshot from within. He saw the commotion and demanded an answer as to what was going on

It was Ned who did the talking, explaining what had happened and informing the sheriff of their intention.

Sheriff Brough attempted to exercise his authority. "There won't be no lynchin', Ned," he said grimly.

"The hell there won't," Ned replied defiantly. "And it's a

hangin', Tom, if'n you wanta look at it that way. She was judged guilty by a eight-man jury who all saw her shoot down Donovan in cold blood."

"I'm still the law here," Brough reminded.

"You *was* the law when Donovan ran this town," Ned shouted. "Now he's dead and you ain't got no say for spit."

The sheriff took a step forward and his hand dropped to his gun belt, the fingers curled. "Ned," he repeated.

The tension of the moment was broken by hoofbeats charging up the main street. All heads turned in the direction of the sound and upon recognizing the silhouettes of George Merrell and Luther armed and ready for a fight, the group encircling Denim swiftly disbanded and started shooting, racing for cover as they did so.

Sheriff Brough swiftly pulled his gun on Ned Randolph, who likewise had his revolver out. But Ned fired the first shot, hitting Brough in the shoulder. The sheriff grabbed his arm and dropped his gun in the dirt. Ned then spun around on the boardwalk and, assuming a wide-legged gunfighter's stance, took aim on George. He got off a series of shots, but the sun was bright in his eyes and each of the bullets missed its target. George leaped off the still-galloping horse and dove behind a water trough, readying his Winchester and firing two rounds that blew Ned Randolph out of his boots. Amid the confusion, Denim scrambled over to Ned's body and retrieved the gun he had taken from her. Then she backed into the saloon and held a position behind the batwings.

She glanced over her shoulder and saw that Joe McDonald had his double-barreled "peacekeeper" cocked and leveled at the men still seated inside the saloon—lest one should change his mind and attempt to join in the melee. Denim nodded gratefully and Joe, though his expression remained set and unpleasant, nodded slightly to her in return.

In the meantime more gunfire erupted from the other cowboys who had taken up varied positions on the street. Luther managed to get off his mount, but in attempting to rush to George his bad leg gave out and he tripped on the road. A bullet zinged by him in the dust. He raised himself on both arms and attempted to crawl for cover. George levered off several quick rounds from his Winchester, then crouch-ran the short distance onto the street to drag Luther to safety behind the water trough. Both were pinned down by the bullets whizzing around them.

George poked his head around the side of the trough and saw that Tom Brough lay dead on the street, probably killed in the crossfire. Denim fired periodically from inside the saloon, but she could not risk exposing herself for more than a second so most of her shots were not aimed and went nowhere. Finally her Colt was empty. Much to her surprise one of the saloon cowboys shouted: "Here, take this," and tossed her his gun. Denim tipped the brim of her Stetson in thanks.

George said to Luther: "Lucky, we're sittin' ducks here. You stay put. I'm gonna try to get to the saloon."

"You'll never make it, Mistuh George," Luther said.

George handed him the rifle.

"You goin' empty-handed?" Luther asked him as if he were crazy.

"Just be ready."

George waited until the gunfire momentarily quieted. Then he leaped up and rolled his tall body onto the boardwalk. One of the cowboys, Nick Lawson, stepped out from his cover with both guns drawn. George hopped to his feet, signaled to Luther, and in a swift move Luther double-hand tossed him the Winchester. George fired a couple of rounds and the cowboy was flung back onto the road, spread-eagle. Seeing George as an open target as he now rushed toward the saloon, two more cowboys made themselves visible and lurched out onto the street. Luther spotted them and blasted away with his revolver, hitting both. They fell and lay writhing in the street.

And then—shots emanating from an unknown source were fired and another cowboy rose from behind a stack of barrels, staggered a few steps into the street, then dropped face-flat with a bullet hole in his forehead. Both George and Luther watched in surprise as three other cowboys were picked off one by one, like targets in a shooting gallery. Whoever was firing seemed to have an eagle-eye view of their positions. Three well-directed single shots. Three dead cowboys. Soon only one very nervous man remained: Ned Randolph's crony Steve Bronson, standing near the mouth of the alley next to the funeral parlor, positioned behind several upright caskets, and he quickly showed himself with his trembling hands raised high. But once on the street, Steve

Bronson impulsively made a dash for a horse tied to a hitching post. Without even thinking to unfasten the reins, he made a leap for the saddle. Another shot rang out and the impact from the bullet somersaulted him back over the horse. He landed dead on the opposite side.

With the smoke cleared, Luther glanced up to where the friendly shooting had originated and noticed that someone was standing in an upstairs open window in the saloon. He only caught a glimpse of the man holding what looked like a short-barreled rifle, who appeared almost as a shadow. Luther would never be able to identify him as he soon disappeared behind the curtains . . . but the man was Ben Straker.

George rushed inside the saloon and Denim grabbed him in an embrace.

"Are you all right?" the girl asked anxiously.

"We got lucky," George breathed. "We owe some stranger a debt of gratitude."

Denim turned to the bartender. "And I owe Joe . . . and that fella over there," she added, indicating the cowboy who had thrown her his gun.

George nodded to the cowboy, and then to the burly barkeep. "I'm indebted to you, Joe."

Joe laid his peacekeeper on the counter. He merely shook his head and sighed.

"Ever'time you come to town, Merrell . . ."

George smiled, then looked back at Denim. She hugged him tightly as their lips came together. They kissed hard, unmindful of those present in the room, thankful for each other's safety.

At that moment Ben Straker appeared at the top of the staircase. He watched as the couple kissed and remained in their embrace, and a look of infinite sadness crossed his face. Without anyone noticing him, he turned and disappeared back down the hall and into his room.

Before they left the saloon George looked at Donovan's lifeless body. He turned to Denim, but didn't utter a word.

Denim never glanced back at the man she had spent her whole life despising.

The man who had died taking a bullet intended for her.

The man who claimed to be her father. . . .

Chapter Sixteen

The Aftermath

With Brock Donovan dead a new law and order would take effect in Prosperity. No longer would the rule of one man dominate. An administration would be elected to govern the affairs of the town fairly. In the meantime a citizen's committee was swiftly formed and one of their first considerations was to change the name of the town. But eventually this was decided against. The town name would stay as is as its hope for the future: that free of its heritage the community would thrive and prosper.

Denim was flush with excitement. This was the morning of the day she was to marry George. In preparation of the event she'd stayed in town overnight with Marie. Marie hadn't been well, with more frequent coughing spasms, but she never let on, enjoying and sharing in Denim's giddy delight. The night before they celebrated with a bottle of claret. Denim only had one glass, but it instantly made her happy. She tried on the special dress that George had bought her for the occasion, and at first did not quite know what to make of herself as she gazed at her reflection in the full-length floor mirror.

"It's like I'm lookin' at a stranger," she told Marie.

But she looked radiant and Marie reassured her of that several times.

Marie had rented a buggy so that she and Denim could ride out to the farm together, where the nuptials would take place that afternoon beside the creek and under the oak tree where the girl had accepted George's proposal. But Denim was fit to bursting to see George and the buggy ride would be too slow. "'Sides," she explained. "Daybreaker's gotta be there just like everyone else."

That morning Denim had on her worn and faded jean outfit. She seemed to appreciate looking at a more recognizable reflection in the mirror.

"Reckon this'll be one of the last times I'll be wearin' these clothes," she said almost regretfully.

"Maybe *that* outfit—thank God," Marie chuckled. "But don't forget you'll be working a farm."

Denim smiled brightly. Her pink face glowed and her dimples were deep in her cheeks.

"Right beside George," she said, enraptured at the thought.

"Nervous?" Marie asked.

Denim shook her head definitely. "Not a mite."

Marie nodded. "I suppose not, after all you've been through since you first came to town. . . . ." She then paused and gave her head a slow shake in wonderment. "You and George Merrell. Who would have ever guessed."

"I love him, Marie," Denim said softly. "And this time I know it's for real."

"I can see that," Marie remarked, gazing into the honesty reflected in Denim's clear blue eyes.

"Well," Denim said with a push of breath, "I'd best be off." She walked to the door, grabbing her Stetson and slapping it against her thigh.

"Oh, honey . . ." Marie said before the girl could leave.

Denim halted. Marie walked over and slipped a simple silver bracelet from her wrist.

"It's not much, but my mother gave it to me back in Canada," Marie explained.

"I—I can't be takin' that," Denim protested.

Marie took Denim's right hand and slid the bracelet onto her wrist. Then she closed her hand over the jewelry and held Denim's wrist gently.

"I can't think of anyone else who I'd want to have it," Marie said tenderly. "I'd always intended to give it to my daughter . . . on her wedding day."

Denim was silent as her head lowered and just the suggestion of tears formed in her eyes. Then she looked up at Marie, smiled, and gave her a long, tight hug. Finally Marie patted her back to urge her along.

"I'll see you right after noon," Marie said. "And I won't be forgetting to bring the dress."

"Thank you, Marie." Though in truth, Denim didn't know whether to be appreciative or disappointed.

Denim walked over to the stable and got her horse from Tom Becker. As she rode out of town she could see how things had changed. Where once she was ignored or met with suspicion, the people who encountered her along the dusty street greeted her with courtesy. Just days before, citizens were afraid of defying Brock Donovan, but now even womenfolk walked easily and with confidence through the town. The change and her small part in enforcing it made Denim feel proud.

The morning air was crisp and once free of the town limits Denim broke Daybreaker into a brisk gallop, her working hand controlling the reins while her gloved hand rested on the pommel.

"Well, fella, next time I'm ridin' you I'll be a married lady. Seems funny to be sayin' that," she said musingly as they entered the trail back to the farm. "Glad you like George . . . an' Luther. They're your family too."

Although it had only been less than a day since she'd seen George, Denim's heart was pounding with anticipation as she urged Daybreaker to pick up speed. She kept thinking that within just a few short hours she would be Mrs. George Merrell. It almost seemed unreal to her—like a dream. She'd hardly ever given thought to being married, but she couldn't be happier at the prospect. . . .

The sharp report of a rifle sounded, echoing through the stillness of the valley. Startled, Daybreaker whinnied and reared at the gunshot and Denim, too engrossed in her thoughts to properly prepare herself, was thrown from the horse. Her head hit against a rock and she lay still.

On a hilly rise just off the trail, concealed by a cluster of underbrush, Ben Straker knelt with his short-barreled "specialty" rifle still in firing position, smoke curling from its end.

It was he who had fired the shot, though for an inexplicable reason known only to himself, at the last minute he had redirected his aim. But he saw that she had fallen and did not move.

Ben had known that today Denim would be returning to the farm—and to the arms of George Merrell. He had loved her . . . and she had come close to loving him, and things could have been different. But he was marked by the life he had chosen, and as such would be denied the happiness that a simple man like George Merrell could embrace. The thought overwhelmed him. Although he'd never met the man he harbored a resentment—even a hatred for George Merrell that betrayed his professional code of refusing to let emotion enter into his work. For he had known—however briefly—joy . . . and love, and because of the rejection of that love he surrendered to a consuming jealousy at another man claiming the girl whom he could never have.

From his vantage point on the sloping hill he stared for a long while at the girl's motionless body until, finally, he stood up and started up the grassy incline to where he'd left his horse. Ben Straker mounted and rode off over the hill. His destiny was set. He had acted on a personal impulse and understood that he would forever be changed by this action. He would go on to accept pay to kill other men until, inevitably, the day would come when he would account for his moment of weakness and fall under the blaze of gunfire . . .

Hank Ferguson was coming up the road in his wagon toward George Merrell's place. George stepped off the porch where he had been sitting with the preacher he had hired to officiate at the wedding, and walked over to greet him. He immediately noticed the troubled look on old Hank's face.

"George, you'd better be ridin' into town," Hank said gravely.

George felt a sudden heaviness in the pit of his gut as he waited for Hank to explain.

"There's been an accident," Hank said, averting his eyes from George.

"Laurie?"

Hank nodded and finally looked at him. "She's at the hotel. Doc Brennan's with her."

George stood momentarily still before he turned and rushed to the back of the house for his horse. Luther came out from the house where he had been preparing food and special treats for the wedding dinner. The wide grin on his face dissolved into a look of concern as he watched George leap upon his mount and race off down the dirt trail.

George broke speed, spurring the horse into town. When he got to the Prosperity Hotel he hopped off the animal without hitching it to the railing post and hurried inside. He stepped over to the desk clerk, who regarded him grimly and told him which room the girl had been taken to. As George climbed the staircase all at once his head cleared and he felt himself starting to succumb to a sense of dread. He realized that he knew nothing about what had happened to Laurie. And he was afraid of what he would find out.

He stood outside the door and listened to the quiet that came from within. Then, bracing himself, he opened the door and quietly walked inside the room. Both Dr. Brennan and Marie were there, standing beside the bed on which Denim lay. They appeared as shadows in the muted light. The curtain was drawn and the room had a gloomy atmosphere. Almost against his will, George directed his eyes toward Denim. She was still dressed in her jean wear and looked to be asleep, her hands folded peacefully over her stomach.

Marie walked over to him, taking both of his hands in hers. Her face was tear-stained and the eye makeup that she had on ran down her cheeks in rivulets. She instantly blamed herself for not insisting that Denim ride with her.

George was too numb to respond with much more than a smile and to give her a comforting pat on the hand.

He gently moved Marie aside and he approached the bed. He stared at Denim for a long while before he finally found the courage to glance over at Dr. Brennan.

Brennan's expression was grave. He lowered his eyes and gave his head an almost imperceptible shake. George responded with an involuntary push of breath.

Brennan said: "She's not in any pain, Merrell."

George's head jerked toward him.

"No," Brennan replied quickly. Then, quietly: "No, she's not . . ."

George lowered his face, then raised it back to the doctor.

"Looks like a riding accident," Brennan explained. "She either fell or was thrown. No marks on her except for a bump on the back of her head. But there's a swelling . . ." The doctor cleared his throat. "Maybe she got a little careless. Just an accident, that's all it looks to be."

Marie felt she had to tell George: "She just wanted to get back to you. She loved you so much."

"Ain't there somethin' . . . ain't there *anything* you can do?" George said to the doctor, struggling to keep his voice strong.

Brennan just opened the palms of his hands in a futile gesture. "I'm sorry, Merrell," was all he said.

Dr. Brennan then gave Marie a slight nudge and they both left the room so that George could be alone with the girl. George's heart had been racing, but now it almost seemed to have stopped. He took the chair next to the bed and lifted Denim's left hand in both of his and tenderly massaged the bent and broken fingers alongside his face.

"Laurie . . . ," George said softly. His eyes were moist with tears. He could never remember crying before, but he felt no shame or embarrassment. His emotion came freely as he'd never felt the kind of love he had for the girl.

He brushed aside the honey-blond hair that had fallen across Denim's face and looked steadily at the girl's still yet serene features. He then leaned forward and pressed a kiss against her slightly parted lips.

Denim's eyes slowly fluttered opened. But when they fell upon the handsome, rugged features of George they widened and instantly sparkled a bright blue.

George hastily wiped the tears from his eyes so that she would not see him cry.

"My girl," George said.

Denim struggled to speak and George moved in a little closer so that he could hear her.

She lowered her long lashes and said: "I'm—sorry . . .'bout today." Her voice was weak, barely audible.

"Don't . . . ," George gently told her.

Denim's expression was troubled. "But we . . . was gonna be married."

"And we will be," George said, giving her hand a light squeeze. "You just gotta get better."

Denim smiled faintly.

"You gotta promise me," George said.

Denim blinked. "I—promise."

They sat quietly for the next few moments. And then Denim said: "could you open the curtain? It's awful dark an' . . . I'd like to take a look at the sunshine."

George nodded. He moved over to the window and parted the curtain so that a bright shaft of daylight opened upon the room. The light poured onto Denim's face and she smiled and shut her eyelids against its warming glow. George stood looking at her for a minute, his expression pained, but his brain overwhelmed by the image of her beauty. He pulled himself together before he went back beside her.

"We'll have a good life together," Denim said to him.

"It'll be a fine life," George replied. He added, "Never thought I was missin' much . . . 'til I met you."

"I'm awful tired," Denim said.

"You get some sleep, honey," George said, choking back the emotion. Against every burning urge, he knew he had to let her go.

"Will you—stay with me?"

George gave his head a slow shake. "I ain't goin' nowhere."

Denim smiled contentedly. She gazed up at George with a look of pure affection.

"I love you, Laurie," George said through trembling lips.

. . . And Denim closed her eyes.

The next morning George rode a wagon back to his farm. Daybreaker was standing in the yard. And moments later Luther rushed outside. The preacher was with him.

"Mistuh George," Luther said. "The horse rode in hisself. I—I knew somethin' was the matter.

George looked at the horse. "Smart animal," he said with a rueful smile.

He slowly climbed down from the wagon and stepped round to the flatbed, stopping briefly to rest a hand against Luther's shoulder as if to steady himself. Luther's heart sank when he saw the casket in back. It was a fine oak box that had been paid for by the residents of Prosperity.

Luther said: "I'm sorry, Mistuh George. I'm mighty sorry."

Later that afternoon they buried her, by the gentle currents of the stream and under the shade of the oak tree where George and Denim were to have been married. A saddened, slow-moving Daybreaker accompanied them. When they departed after the preacher spoke a few words, the loyal horse refused to follow. He stayed by the grave.

George sat out on the porch that evening. He smoked a cigarette while listening to the peaceful quiet and gazing out at a clear sky that was alive with stars, each twinkling with an unnatural brilliance.

Shortly, Luther came out to join him.

They sat quietly together, until George sighed. Luther turned to him and noticed the sadness still reflected in his friend's eyes.

But George said: "Reckon if a man finds the love I had with Laurie, then he ain't lacked for anythin'."

Luther looked up at the wide skies and pointed a finger to the stars. "Know she's up there, Mistuh George. She's up there lookin' out for yuh."

George managed a brave smile.

Luther paused before adding: "And so am I."

And the two men sat in silent reflection throughout the night, each with his own thoughts and shared memories of the girl known as Denim Ryder.